Right You Are If You Think You Are

LUIGI PIRANDELLO

Translated by Stanley Appelbaum

❧

DOVER PUBLICATIONS, INC.
Mineola, New York

DOVER THRIFT EDITIONS

GENERAL EDITOR: STANLEY APPELBAUM

This Dover Thrift Edition may be used in its entirety, adaptation or in any other way for theatrical productions and performances, professional and amateur, in the United States, without fee, permission or acknowledgment. (This may not apply outside of the United States, as copyright conditions may vary.)

Bibliographical Note

The present volume, first published by Dover Publications, Inc., in 1997, consists of a new English translation of Luigi Pirandello's play *Così è (se vi pare)* and a new Note, both by Stanley Appelbaum. See the Note (opposite) for data on the first publication of the Italian text.

Library of Congress Cataloging-in-Publication Data

Pirandello, Luigi, 1867–1936.
[Così è (se vi pare).   English]
Right you are if you think you are / Luigi Pirandello ; translated by Stanley Appelbaum.
     p.   cm.
ISBN 0-486-29576-1 (pbk.)
I. Appelbaum, Stanley.   II. Title.
PQ4835.I7C613   1997
852'.912—dc20
                     96-36041
                     CIP

Manufactured in the United States of America
Dover Publications, Inc., 31 East 2nd Street, Mineola, N.Y. 11501

Note

SICILIAN-BORN Luigi Pirandello (1867–1936; winner of the 1934 Nobel Prize for literature) was already in his fifties, and already well known in Italy as a poet, essayist, novelist and author of short stories, before he started writing the plays that made him world-famous. His first great theatrical success, *Così è (se vi pare)* [Right You Are If You Think You Are],[1] was first produced in Milan on June 18, 1917, by the Compagnia di Virgilio Talli. It was first published in the issues of January 1 and January 16, 1918, of the Rome-based journal *Nuova Antologia di Lettere, Scienze ed Arti*,[2] with the subtitle "Parabola in tre atti" [Parable in Three Acts]. Later in 1918 it was included in the first of the collected-play volumes Pirandello called *Maschere nude* [Naked Masks], with a very slightly modified text that is the basis of the present translation.[3]

Like a number of Pirandello's plays, *Right You Are* is based on one of his own short stories, in this case "La signora Frola e il signor Ponza, suo genero" [Mrs. Frola and Mr. Ponza, Her Son-in-Law], first published in 1917. The entire content of Acts Two and Three is new to the play, and it is only in the play that the townspeople (as opposed to Mrs. Frola and Mr. Ponza) are given names, ranks and characterizations. An especially new character is Laudisi, the spokesman for the author's own attitudes and viewpoints (the kind of role called a *raisonneur* in turn-of-the-cen-

---

[1]This, the most widely known English version of the title, has been adopted here, although the play has been translated and produced under a variety of titles in Britain and the U.S. The actual meaning of the Italian title, slightly expanded and paraphrased, is: "That's the truth of the matter—*if* you happen to think so."

[2]Sixth Series, January–February 1918, Vol. CXCIII.

[3]Eric Bentley's translation of 1952 seems to reflect some additional, barely perceptible changes possibly made by Pirandello for an edition of 1922.

tury French drama). The most startlingly new feature is the introduction of the veiled woman at the end, which to some extent moves the action from a realistic to a symbolic plane (she resembles the sacred, untouchable veiled images of Truth in old legends).

The town in which the action takes place is the capital of a *provincia*, one of the main administrative subdivisions of Italy, something like a state in the U.S. or a county in England. Agazzi is a member of the council that governs the *provincia*; in the present translation, he is generally referred to obliquely as "Councilman" and called "Your Honor" in formal direct address. The chief administrator of a *provincia* is a *prefetto*; the present translation uses the term "Governor" (although a *prefetto* is not the locally elected head of a sovereign state, but a representative of the central government in Rome), with the formal direct address "Your Excellency." Producers or readers may feel free to substitute the more precise term "Prefect" if they wish.

Right You Are is one of the principal statements of some prevalent Pirandellian themes: the difficulty of separating reality from fantasy, the fluidity of personal identity and the relativity of truth. Incidentally, Pirandello had a very painful personal experience of insanity in his family: his wife suffered a nervous breakdown in 1903 and for years persecuted him with morbid jealousy until she had to be institutionalized in 1919.

Contents

Characters

LAMBERTO LAUDISI
MRS. FROLA
MR. PONZA, her son-in-law
MRS. PONZA
COUNCILMAN AGAZZI
MRS. AMALIA AGAZZI, his wife and Lamberto Laudisi's sister
DINA, their daughter
MRS. SIRELLI
MR. SIRELLI
The Governor of the province
Police Commissioner Centuri
MRS. CINI
MRS. NENNI
A butler in the Agazzi home
Other ladies and gentlemen

Place and time:
In a provincial capital. Present day.

ACT ONE

Living room in the home of Councilman Agazzi. Principal door in the back; side doors at right and left.

SCENE ONE

Amalia, Dina, Laudisi.

As the curtain rises, Lamberto Laudisi is pacing the room in a state of annoyance. About forty years old, slender and brisk, well dressed without affectation, he is wearing a violet jacket with black lapels and black piping.

LAUDISI: So he's gone to see the Governor about it?

AMALIA (*about forty-five, gray hair; her manner clearly shows the feeling of self-importance she derives from her husband's rank in society. But she also indicates that, if it were up to her, she could play the part herself and would then often behave quite differently*): Would you believe it, Lamberto, all on account of a man who's his subordinate!

LAUDISI: A subordinate when your husband sits on the Governor's council—but not at home!

DINA (*nineteen; behaves as though convinced she is much wiser than her mother and even than her father; but this trait is softened by her lively, youthful grace*): Even though he moved his mother-in-law in right next to us, on the same floor?

LAUDISI: Didn't he have a right to? It was a vacant apartment and he leased it for his mother-in-law. Or is a mother-in-law perhaps obliged to come and call on (*exaggeratedly, purposely draw-*

1

ing out the words) the wife and daughter of one of her son-in-law's superiors?

AMALIA: Who says she's obliged? As I remember it, *we*, Dina and I, were the ones who went on our own to call on that lady, and *we weren't received*.

LAUDISI: And why has your husband now gone to the Governor? To put official pressure on her to observe etiquette toward you?

AMALIA: To make proper amends to us, if you want to call it that! Because you just don't leave two ladies that way, standing in front of your door like a couple of statues!

LAUDISI: That's going too far! Aren't people allowed to stay home and mind their own business?

AMALIA: But you totally disregard the fact that *we* were the ones who took it on ourselves to be polite—to a stranger!

DINA: Uncle, calm down, please! If you want, we'll be honest: there! we admit that our politeness was out of curiosity. But, tell me, don't you find that natural?

LAUDISI: Natural, yes: because the two of you are totally idle.

DINA: Come now, Uncle! Let's say you are sitting there, paying no attention to what anyone else is doing around you. Fine. I come along. And here, right on this end table that's standing in front of you, with no expression on my face—no, let's say with an expression like a criminal's, like *that* man's—I plunk down—what should I say?—a pair of the cook's shoes!

LAUDISI: (*in an outburst*): What have the cook's shoes got to do with anything?

DINA: (*immediately*): There, you see? You're surprised! You think it's bizarre, and you immediately ask me why.

LAUDISI: (*surprised, with a cold smile, but quickly recovering*): Darling! You're very clever; but, remember, you're talking to *me*. You've just put the cook's shoes down on this table for no other reason than to arouse my curiosity; and surely—since you did it on purpose—you can't blame me for asking you: "Darling, what are the cook's shoes doing here?" Now you need to prove to me that this Mr. Ponza—a boorish scoundrel, as your father calls him—was also doing it on purpose when he moved his mother-in-law in next to us!

DINA: All right! So it wasn't on purpose. But you can't deny that he lives in such a bizarre way that it's perfectly understandable if he provokes the curiosity of the whole town. Listen. He comes here. He rents an apartment on the top floor of that dreary tenement out there at the edge of town, near the market gardens. Have you seen it? I mean, inside?

LAUDISI: I suppose you've been to see it!

DINA: Yes, Uncle! With Mother. And not just us, you know. Everyone's been to see it. There's a courtyard—so dark! it's like a well!—with an iron railing all the way up, running along the gallery on the top floor, and with ever so many baskets hanging down from it on strings.

LAUDISI: And so?

DINA   (*surprised and indignant*): He's marooned his wife up there!

AMALIA: And brought his mother-in-law here, next door to us!

LAUDISI: But the mother-in-law is in a fine apartment, in the heart of town!

AMALIA: Thanks! And he forces her to live away from her daughter?

LAUDISI: Who told you so? Can't it rather be the mother's wish, in order to have more freedom?

DINA: No, no! Oh, Uncle! Everyone knows it's his doing!

AMALIA: Listen, you can understand it if a daughter who gets married leaves her mother's home and goes to live with her husband; even in another town. But when a poor mother, who can't bear to live far away from her daughter, follows her and, in a town where both of them are strangers, is forced to live somewhere else, you surely must admit that *that* is *not* easy to understand!

LAUDISI: So! What lazy minds you have! Is it so hard to imagine that, either through her fault, or through his fault—or even without anyone being at fault—there may be such incompatibility of characters that, even under these circumstances . . .

DINA   (*interrupting him in surprise*): What, Uncle? Between a mother and daughter?

LAUDISI: Why do you say between a mother and daughter?

AMALIA: Because there's none between the other two! He and she are always together!

DINA: A mother-in-law and son-in-law! *That's* what amazes everybody!

AMALIA: He comes here every evening to keep his mother-in-law company.

DINA: He even comes once or twice during the day.

LAUDISI: Do you perhaps suspect that they're lovers, the mother-in-law and son-in-law?

DINA: What are you saying? A poor old lady!

AMALIA: But he never brings along her daughter! He never brings his wife with him to see her mother, never, never!

LAUDISI: Maybe the poor woman is sick . . . maybe she can't leave her house . . .

DINA: No, no! The mother goes *there* . . .

AMALIA: She goes there, yes! But only to look at her from a distance! It's known for an absolute fact that that poor mother is forbidden to walk up into her daughter's house!

DINA: She can only talk to her from the courtyard!

AMALIA: From the courtyard, do you hear?

DINA: To her daughter, who looks out of the gallery window up there, as far away as if she were in heaven! That poor woman enters the courtyard, pulls on the basket string and rings the bell up above; her daughter looks out, and she talks to her from down below, from the bottom of that well, straining her neck like this! Imagine! And she doesn't even really see her, because she's blinded by the light that filters down.

A knock is heard at the door and the Butler appears.

BUTLER: Pardon!

AMALIA: Who is it?

BUTLER: Mr. and Mrs. Sirelli with another lady.

AMALIA: Oh, show them in.

The Butler bows and exits.

SCENE TWO

Mr. and Mrs. Sirelli, Mrs. Cini and the foregoing.

AMALIA   (*to Mrs. Sirelli*): How good to see you!

MRS. SIRELLI   (*plump, sprightly, still young, dressed with overdone provincial elegance; burning with unassuaged curiosity; rude to her husband*): I took the liberty of bringing along my good friend Mrs. Cini, who wanted so much to meet you.

AMALIA: A pleasure. Please sit down, everybody. (*Introducing:*) This is my daughter Dina. My brother, Lamberto Laudisi.

SIRELLI   (*mostly bald, about forty, fat, brilliantined, with claims to sartorial elegance, wearing highly polished shoes that squeak; in greeting*): Mrs. Agazzi. Miss Agazzi.

He shakes hands with Laudisi.

MRS. SIRELLI: Ah, Mrs. Agazzi, we have come here as if to the fountain of knowledge. We're two poor women parched for news.

AMALIA: News of what, ladies?

MRS. SIRELLI: You know—about that wretched new secretary in the Governor's office. No one in town is talking about anything else!

MRS. CINI   (*a foolish old woman, full of active malice disguised as naïveté*): All of us women are curious, so curious that . . . we can't stand it!

AMALIA: But, believe me, Mrs. Cini, we don't know more about him than anyone else!

SIRELLI   (*to his wife, as if he had won a victory*): Didn't I tell you? They know just as much as I do, and maybe even less! (*Then, turning to the others:*) For example, do you know the real reason why this poor mother can't go visit her daughter at home?

AMALIA: I was just talking about that with my brother.

LAUDISI: I think you've all gone crazy!

DINA   (*quickly, so they won't pay attention to her uncle*): Because they say her son-in-law won't let her.

MRS. CINI   (*sorrowfully*): That's not all, Miss Agazzi!

MRS. SIRELLI (*without a pause*): That's not all! He does more than that!

SIRELLI (*with a preliminary hand gesture to assure their attention*): News flash, just now ascertained: (*almost syllable by syllable:*) He keeps her locked up!

AMALIA: His mother-in-law?

SIRELLI: No: his wife!

MRS. SIRELLI: His wife! His wife!

MRS. CINI   (*sorrowfully*): Under lock and key!

DINA: You hear, Uncle? And you want to excuse . . .

SIRELLI   (*amazed*): What? You want to excuse that monster?

LAUDISI: But I don't want to excuse him at all! What I'm saying is that your curiosity (I beg the ladies to forgive me) is intolerable—if for no other reason, because it's pointless.

SIRELLI: Pointless?

LAUDISI: Pointless!—Pointless, ladies!

MRS. CINI: For us to want to find out?

LAUDISI: Find out what, pray tell? What can we really know about other people? Who they are . . . what they're like . . . what they do . . . why they do it . . .

MRS. SIRELLI: By asking for news, for information . . .

LAUDISI: But if there's one lady who ought to be abreast of everything of that sort, it must surely be you, Mrs. Sirelli, with a husband like yours, always so well informed on all counts!

SIRELLI (*trying to interrupt*): Excuse me, excuse me . . .

MRS. SIRELLI: No, dear, listen: that's the truth! (*Addressing Amalia:*) The truth, Mrs. Agazzi: with my husband, who always says he knows everything, I never manage to know a thing.

SIRELLI: Naturally! She's never satisfied with what I tell her! She always suspects that things aren't the way I said they were. In fact, she maintains that things *can't* be the way I said they were. She even ends up believing the opposite on principle!

MRS. SIRELLI (*to her husband*): Come on, now, some of those stories you tell me . . .

LAUDISI (*laughing out loud*): Ha, ha, ha! . . . May I, Mrs. Sirelli? I'd like to answer your husband. My dear man, how can you expect your wife to be satisfied with the things you tell her if you—as is only natural—tell them to her as *you* see them?

MRS. SIRELLI: As they absolutely cannot be!

LAUDISI: Oh, no, Mrs. Sirelli, permit me to state that in this case *you* are wrong! Be assured that, for your husband, things *are* as he tells them to you.

SIRELLI: And as they really are! As they really are!

MRS. SIRELLI: Not a bit! You're constantly mistaken!

SIRELLI: You're the mistaken one, let me tell you! I don't make mistakes!

LAUDISI: No, no, good people! Neither of you is mistaken. May I go on? I'll prove it to you. (*He gets up and takes a stand in the center of the room.*) You both see me here.—You see me, don't you?

SIRELLI: Sure, I do!

LAUDISI: No, no; don't say it so fast, my friend. Come over here, come over here.

SIRELLI (*looks at him with a smile, puzzled, a little confused, as if not wishing to participate in some joke he doesn't understand*): Why?

MRS. SIRELLI   (*urging him on, with irritation in her voice*): Oh, go on over there.

LAUDISI   (*to Sirelli, who has approached him hesitantly*): You see me? Take a better look at me. Touch me.

MRS. SIRELLI   (*to her husband, who hesitates to touch him*): Well, touch him!

LAUDISI   (*to Sirelli, who has raised one hand to touch him lightly on the shoulder*): Good, bravo! Now, you're as sure about touching me as about seeing me, right?

SIRELLI: I'd say so.

LAUDISI: You can't doubt your own senses, naturally!—Go back to your seat.

MRS. SIRELLI   (*to her husband, who is still standing foolishly in front of Laudisi*): There's no point in your standing there blinking your eyes; sit down again!

LAUDISI   (*to Mrs. Sirelli, once her husband has returned to his seat in bewilderment*): Now, if you don't mind, you come here, Mrs. Sirelli. (*Suddenly, before she can do so:*) No, no, I will come to you. (*He walks in front of her and drops down on one knee.*) You see me, right? Raise your hand; touch me. (*And as Mrs. Sirelli, seated, places one hand on his shoulder, he bends over to kiss it, saying:*) Dear little hand!

SIRELLI: Hey there, hey there!

LAUDISI: Pay no attention to him!—Are you also as sure about touching me as about seeing me? You can't doubt your own senses.—But, for heaven's sake, don't tell your husband, or my sister, or my niece or Mrs.—

MRS. CINI   (*prompting him*): Cini.

LAUDISI: Mrs. Cini—*how* you see me, or else all four of them will tell you you're mistaken, even though you're not mistaken at all! Because I really am as you see me.—But, dear lady, that does not negate the fact that I am also in reality just as I am seen by your husband, my sister, my niece and Mrs.—

MRS. CINI   (*prompting him*): Cini.

LAUDISI: Mrs. Cini—and that they, too, are not at all mistaken.

MRS. SIRELLI: But how can you possibly change from one to the other?

LAUDISI: But of course I change, Mrs. Sirelli! You don't change?

MRS. SIRELLI   (*hurriedly*): No, no, no, no! I assure you that in my eyes I don't change at all!

LAUDISI: Nor in mine, believe me! And I say that you're all mistaken if you don't see me as I see myself! But that does not negate the fact that that is quite a presumption on my part, as it is on yours, my dear lady.

SIRELLI: But, excuse me, what is all this mumbo-jumbo meant to prove?

LAUDISI: You think it proves nothing? Oh, my! I see you all here so intent on finding out who other people are and how things stand, as if other people and things had to be either one way or another.

MRS. SIRELLI: So, in your opinion, it's never possible to learn the truth?

MRS. CINI: If we can't even believe what we see and touch!

LAUDISI: Yes, do believe it, Mrs. Cini! But I say to you: also respect what the others see and touch, even if it's the opposite of what *you* see and touch.

MRS. SIRELLI: Listen! I'm shutting you out! I'm not going to talk to you any more! I don't want to go crazy!

LAUDISI: No, no! That's enough! All of you go on talking about Mrs. Frola and Mr. Ponza, her son-in-law: I won't interrupt you any more.

AMALIA: Thank God for that! And Lamberto dear, wouldn't it be better if you went into another room?

DINA: Yes, do, Uncle; go, go!

LAUDISI: No, why should I? I enjoy hearing you talk. I'll keep quiet, rest assured. At the most, I'll give a little laugh inside; and if a louder laugh escapes me, you'll surely forgive me.

MRS. SIRELLI: And to think that we came here for information . . . — But, tell me, Mrs. Agazzi, isn't your husband a superior of this Mr. Ponza?

AMALIA: The office is one thing and home is another, Mrs. Sirelli.

MRS. SIRELLI: I understand; that's right! — But haven't you even tried to see the mother-in-law, who lives right next door to you?

DINA: Of course we did! Twice, Mrs. Sirelli!

MRS. CINI (*with a start; then, greedily and intently*): So, then! So you've spoken to her!

AMALIA: We weren't received, Mrs. Cini!

SIRELLI, MRS. SIRELLI, MRS. CINI: Oh! Oh! — Just think of it!

DINA: This morning again . . .

AMALIA: The first time, we waited more than fifteen minutes outside the door. No one came to open, and we couldn't even leave a calling card.—Today we tried again . . .

DINA   (*with a gesture expressive of fear*): *He* came to open!

MRS. SIRELLI: What a face! Yes! He really has an evil one! He's upset the whole town with that face! And then, always dressed in black like that . . . All three wear black, even his wife, right? The daughter?

SIRELLI   (*disgusted*): But no one has even seen the daughter! I've told you so a thousand times! She probably wears black, too . . .— They're from a tiny place in Marsica, in the Abruzzi—

AMALIA: Which was totally destroyed, it seems—

SIRELLI: Wiped out, razed to the ground, by the latest earthquake.

DINA: They lost all their relatives, people say.

MRS. CINI   (*eager to resume the interrupted train of thought*): Well? Well? So he opened the door?

AMALIA: The moment I saw him in front of me, with that face, my voice failed me and I could just barely tell him we had come to call on his mother-in-law. Not a word, do you hear? Not even a thank you.

DINA: Oh, but he *did* make a bow.

AMALIA: Just very slightly . . . like this, with his head.

DINA: With his eyes, rather, you should say! Those are the eyes of a wild animal, not a man.

MRS. CINI   (*as above*): And then? What did he say then?

DINA: He was quite embarrassed—

AMALIA: Quite muddled; he told us his mother-in-law was indisposed . . . that he thanked us for our attentions . . . and he just stood there, on the threshold, waiting for us to leave.

DINA: How mortifying!

SIRELLI: The bad manners of a lout! Ah, you may be sure that it's his doing! Maybe he keeps his mother-in-law locked up, too!

MRS. SIRELLI: That takes nerve! To a lady who's the wife of one of his superiors!

AMALIA: Oh, this time my husband got really angry: he took it as a serious lack of respect and he's gone to vent his feelings to the Governor, and ask for satisfaction.

DINA: Oh, what do you know, here's Father now!

SCENE THREE

Councilman Agazzi, the foregoing.

AGAZZI　(*fifty years old, red-haired, tousled, bearded, gold-rimmed glasses, imperious and petulant*): Oh, Sirelli! (*He approaches the sofa, bows and takes Mrs. Sirelli's hand.*) Mrs. Sirelli!

AMALIA　(*introducing him to Mrs. Cini*): My husband—Mrs. Cini.

AGAZZI　(*bows, takes her hand*): A great pleasure. (*Then, addressing his wife and daughter almost solemnly:*) I want you to know that in a few moments Mrs. Frola will be here.

MRS. SIRELLI　(*clapping her hands, exulting*): Ah, she's coming? She's coming here?

AGAZZI:　Of course! Could I tolerate such barefaced rudeness to my household, to my ladies?

SIRELLI:　Yes. We were just saying that very thing!

MRS. SIRELLI:　And you would have done well to use that opportunity—

AGAZZI　(*forestalling her*): To notify the Governor of all that's being said in town about that gentleman? Well, have no doubts: that's what I did!

SIRELLI:　Oh, good, good!

MRS. CINI:　Unexplainable things! Truly unimaginable!

AMALIA:　Downright savage! Do you know he keeps them both locked up?

DINA:　No, Mother. We don't know yet if it's true for his mother-in-law!

MRS. SIRELLI:　But for his wife, it's certain!

SIRELLI:　And the Governor?

AGAZZI:　Yes . . . Well . . . He was very . . . very shocked . . .

SIRELLI:　Good!

AGAZZI:　He had had some word of it, as well, and . . . and now he, too, sees the chance to clear up this mystery, to find out the truth.

LAUDISI　(*laughs out loud*): Ha, ha, ha, ha!

AMALIA:　All we needed now was for you to laugh.

AGAZZI:　Why is he laughing?

MRS. SIRELLI:　Because he says it's impossible to uncover the truth!

SCENE FOUR

Butler, the foregoing, then Mrs. Frola.

BUTLER   (*appearing on the threshold and announcing*): Pardon. Mrs. Frola.
SIRELLI: Oh, here she is.
AGAZZI: Now we'll see if it isn't possible, my dear Lamberto!
MRS. SIRELLI: Fine! Oh, I'm really happy!
AMALIA   (*rising*): Shall we ask her in?
AGAZZI: No, please sit down. Wait for her to come in. Everyone seated. We must be seated. (*To the Butler:*) Show her in.

The Butler exits. Shortly afterward Mrs. Frola enters and everyone rises. Mrs. Frola is a neat little old lady, modest, very affable, with a great sadness in her eyes that is softened by a constant sweet smile on her lips. Amalia goes up to her and offers her hand.

AMALIA: Please come in, Mrs. Frola. (*Holding her hand, she introduces the others:*) My good friend Mrs. Sirelli. Mrs. Cini. My husband. Mr. Sirelli. My daughter Dina. My brother, Lamberto Laudisi. Please sit down, Mrs. Frola.
MRS. FROLA: I'm very sorry and I apologize for having failed in my duties up to now.—You, Mrs. Agazzi, honored me so graciously with a call, when it was for me to come first.
AMALIA: Between neighbors, Mrs. Frola, it makes no difference whose turn it is first. All the more so because you, alone here, a stranger, might have needed . . .
MRS. FROLA: Thank you, thank you . . . too kind . . .
MRS. SIRELLI: You're alone in town, Mrs. Frola?
MRS. FROLA: No, I have a married daughter; she, too, came here recently.
SIRELLI: Your son-in-law is secretary in the Governor's office: Mr. Ponza, correct?
MRS. FROLA: Exactly. And (*to Agazzi:*) you will pardon me, I hope, Your Honor, and pardon my son-in-law, too.
AGAZZI: To tell the truth, Mrs. Frola, I *was* somewhat disturbed—
MRS. FROLA   (*interrupting him*): You're right! You're right! But you must excuse him! Believe me, we are still so disoriented by our misfortune.

AMALIA: Of course! You had that great catastrophe!

MRS. SIRELLI: You lost relatives?

MRS. FROLA: Oh, all of them! All, Mrs. Sirelli. There's hardly a trace left of our little town; it's just a heap of abandoned ruins in the midst of the countryside.

SIRELLI: Yes, we heard!

MRS. FROLA: I had only a sister left, and she too had a daughter, but of marrying age.   For my poor son-in-law the disaster was much greater. His mother, two brothers, a sister and then his brother-in-law, sisters-in-law, two nephews.

SIRELLI: A hecatomb!

MRS. FROLA: And they are disasters that you never get over! You remain dazed by it all!

AMALIA: Naturally!

MRS. SIRELLI: From one moment to the next! A person could go crazy!

MRS. FROLA: You no longer think about anything else. You fail in your duties without intending to, Your Honor.

AGAZZI: Oh, please say no more about it, Mrs. Frola.

AMALIA: It was also because we knew of that disaster that my daughter and I came to call on you first.

MRS. SIRELLI   (*seething with impatience*): Yes! Knowing that you were so all alone, Mrs. Frola!—But forgive me, if I dare to ask how it is that, having your daughter here, after a disaster like that . . . (*hesitant after having led up to it so skillfully:*) It would seem to me . . . such a tragedy would instill in the survivors the need to stick together—

MRS. FROLA   (*following her; to relieve her of her embarrassment*): You wonder how it is that I'm living by myself, isn't that it?

SIRELLI: Yes, that's just it. To be perfectly honest, it seems strange.

MRS. FROLA   (*sadly*): Oh, I understand. (*Then, as if attempting a way out:*) But . . . you know, my feeling is that, when a son or daughter marries, they should be left to themselves, to make a life of their own, you see.

LAUDISI: Wonderful! Perfectly reasonable! Because it must of necessity be a different life, in the new relationship with the wife or husband.

MRS. SIRELLI: But excuse me, Laudisi, not to the point of shutting your mother out of your new life!

LAUDISI: Who said anything about shutting out? What we're talking about now—if I understood correctly—is a mother who understands that her daughter cannot and should not remain tied to her as previously, now that she has another life to live.

MRS. FROLA   (*with intense gratitude*): There, that's just it, sir! Thank you! That's exactly what I meant to say!

MRS. CINI: But your daughter, I imagine, probably comes here often to keep you company.

MRS. FROLA   (*uncomfortably*): Yes . . . yes, we see each other, certainly . . .

SIRELLI   (*quickly*): But your daughter never goes out of the house! At least, no one has ever seen her!

MRS. CINI: Maybe she has to tend to her children!

MRS. FROLA   (*quickly*): No, there's no child yet. And maybe, by this time, she won't have any. She's been married for seven years now. She's kept busy in the house, certainly.—But that's not the reason. (*She smiles sadly, and, trying another way out, she adds:*) You know, we—we women—in little towns, are accustomed to stay at home all the time.

AGAZZI: Even when there's a mother for them to visit? A mother who no longer lives with them?

AMALIA: But you must surely go yourself to see your daughter!

MRS. FROLA   (*quickly*): Oh, of course! Naturally! I go there once or twice a day!

SIRELLI: And once or twice a day you climb up all those stairs, up to the top floor of that tenement?

MRS. FROLA   (*anguished, still trying to laugh off the torture of this cross-examination*): Oh, no; actually, I don't climb up. You're right, sir; it would be too hard for me. I don't climb up. My daughter looks out on the side facing the courtyard and . . . and we see each other, we talk to each other.

MRS. SIRELLI: Nothing but that? Oh! You never see her close up?

DINA   (*hugging her mother's neck*): I, as a daughter, wouldn't ask my mother to climb up ninety or a hundred steps on my account; but I wouldn't be content to see her and talk to her from a distance, without embracing her, without feeling her near me.

MRS. FROLA   (*extremely upset and embarrassed*): You're right! Oh, well, I have to tell you.—I wouldn't want you to have the wrong idea about my daughter, to think she has no love or regard for me. Or even to have the wrong idea about me, as her mother . . . Ninety or a hundred steps shouldn't be an obstacle to a mother, even if she's old and tired, when at the top of them she has the reward of being able to clasp her own daughter to her heart.

MRS. SIRELLI   (*triumphantly*): Ah, there! We were saying that, Mrs. Frola! There must be a reason!

AMALIA   (*purposefully*): There *is*, you see, Lamberto? There *is* a reason!

SIRELLI   (*quickly*): Your son-in-law, eh?

MRS. FROLA: Oh, no, for heaven's sake, don't think badly of him! He's such a good young man! You can't imagine how kind he is! What tender and delicate affection he has for me, full of thoughtfulness! Not even to mention the love and solicitude he has for my daughter. Oh, believe me, I couldn't have wanted a better husband for her.

MRS. SIRELLI: But . . . in that case?

MRS. CINI: Then he's not the reason!

AGAZZI: Of course he is! At least, I find it unthinkable that he should forbid his wife to visit her mother, or the mother to walk up to their home to spend some time with her daughter!

MRS. FROLA: Forbid it? No! I didn't say anything about his forbidding us to do so! We ourselves, Your Honor, my daughter and I: we refrain from it, of our own accord, believe me, out of regard for him.

AGAZZI: Excuse me, how could he be annoyed? Over what? I can't see it!

MRS. FROLA: Not annoyed, Your Honor.—It's a sentiment . . . a sentiment, ladies, that may be hard to understand. But when you understand it, believe me, it's no longer hard to accept; although, without a doubt, it entails a heavy sacrifice for both me and my daughter.

AGAZZI: You'll admit, Mrs. Frola, that all this you're telling us is strange, to say the least.

SIRELLI: Yes, and of a nature to arouse and justify curiosity.

AGAZZI: And, I would add, even some suspicion.

MRS. FROLA: Of him? No, for God's sake, don't say that! What suspicion, Your Honor?

AGAZZI: None! Don't get upset. I said that it was *possible* to have a suspicion.

MRS. FROLA: No, no! And about what? We all live in perfect harmony! Both my daughter and I are contented, as contented as can be.

MRS. SIRELLI: Could it be jealousy?

MRS. FROLA: Of her mother? Jealousy? I don't think it can be called that. Although I really couldn't say.—It's like this: he wants his wife's heart all to himself, to such an extent that the love that my daughter must have for her mother (and he admits that, of course—how could he not?)—he wants even that love to reach me by way of him, through his agency—that's it!

AGAZZI: Oh, excuse me! To me that seems like pure and simple cruelty!

MRS. FROLA: No, no, not cruelty! Don't say cruelty, Your Honor! It's something else, believe me! I can't manage to express it . . . —His nature, that's it! No . . . Maybe, oh, Lord, it's even a kind of sickness, if you wish. It's like an overabundance of love—which is enclosed—yes, that's it, exclusive—in which his wife must live, without ever stepping outside it, and which no one else must enter.

DINA: Not even her mother?

SIRELLI: Downright selfishness, I'd call it!

MRS. FROLA: Perhaps. But a selfishness that makes a total offering of itself, big as the whole world, to his own wife! Actually, the selfishness would be on my part if I wanted to break into that closed universe of love, when I know that my daughter is living happily inside it; completely worshipped!—That ought to be enough for a mother, don't you think so, ladies?—Anyway, since I see my daughter and talk to her . . . (*with a gracious spurt of confidentiality:*) The basket that I tug on in the courtyard there always carries back and forth a little note, with the news of the day.—That's enough for me.—And by this time I'm used to it; resigned, if you prefer! It no longer hurts me.

AMALIA: Well, after all, if you two are contented!

MRS. FROLA   (*rising*): Oh, yes! I told you so. Because he's so good—believe me!—he couldn't be more so!—We all have our faults, and we need to understand each other's mutually. (*She takes leave of Amalia:*) Mrs. Agazzi. (*She takes leave of Mrs. Sirelli and Mrs. Cini, then Dina; then, addressing Councilman Agazzi:*) I hope you've forgiven me . . .

AGAZZI: Oh, Mrs. Frola, don't mention it! We're most grateful to you for your visit.

MRS. FROLA   (*nods to Sirelli and Laudisi, then, addressing Amalia*): No, please . . . stay here, please, Mrs. Agazzi . . . don't put yourself to any trouble . . .

AMALIA: Not at all, it's only right of me, Mrs. Frola.

Mrs. Frola exits, accompanied by Amalia, who returns at once.

SIRELLI: Well, what about that? Are you all satisfied with the explanation?

AGAZZI: What explanation? Who knows what mystery is at the bottom of all this?

MRS. SIRELLI: And who knows how that poor mother's heart must be aching?

DINA: And the daughter's too, I'd swear!

Pause.

MRS. CINI   (*from the corner of the room, where she has crept to hide her tears; breaking out shrilly*): The tears were trembling in her voice!

AMALIA: Yes! When she said that climbing a hundred steps would be nothing to her, if she could only clasp her daughter to her heart!

LAUDISI: As for me, what I observed above all was an attempt—I'd even say a diligent eagerness—to protect her son-in-law from any suspicion!

MRS. SIRELLI: What do you mean? My heavens, she didn't know how to excuse him!

SIRELLI: Excuse him! For his violence? For his barbarity?

SCENE FIVE

Butler, the foregoing, then Mr. Ponza.

BUTLER   (*appearing on the threshold*): Your Honor, Mr. Ponza is here and requests you to receive him.

MRS. SIRELLI: Oh, it's him!

General surprise and gestures of anxious curiosity, coming close to alarm.

AGAZZI: Received by me?

BUTLER: Yes, sir. That's what he said.

MRS. SIRELLI: For mercy's sake, receive him, Your Honor!—I'm almost afraid, but I'm so curious to see him up close, the monster!

AMALIA: But what could he want?

AGAZZI: We'll find out. Sit down, everybody. We must be seated. (*To the Butler:*) Show him in.

The Butler bows and exits. Soon thereafter Mr. Ponza enters. Stocky, dark, with an almost brutal look, dressed all in black, thick black hair, low forehead, big black mustache. He keeps on clenching his fists and speaks with an effort, in fact with barely restrained violence. From time to time he wipes the sweat from his face with a black-edged handkerchief. When he speaks, his eyes remain constantly hard, fixed, gloomy.

AGAZZI: Come in, step in, Mr. Ponza! (*Introducing him:*) The new secretary, Mr. Ponza: my wife—Mrs. Sirelli—Mrs. Cini—my daughter—Mr. Sirelli—my brother-in-law Laudisi. Have a seat.

PONZA: Thank you. Just a moment and I'll be out of your way.

AGAZZI: Do you wish to speak with me privately?

PONZA: No, I can . . . I can say this to one and all. In fact . . . It's . . . it's a dutiful declaration on my part.

AGAZZI: Do you mean with regard to your mother-in-law's call? You don't need to, because—

PONZA: It's not about that, Your Honor. In fact, I must inform you that Mrs. Frola, my mother-in-law, would undoubtedly have come before your wife and daughter were kind enough to honor her with their call, if I hadn't done everything in my power to prevent her from doing so, since I can't allow her to make calls or receive any.

AGAZZI   (*with strong resentment*): Why not, in heaven's name?

PONZA   (*becoming more and more upset, despite his efforts to control himself*): My mother-in-law must have spoken to you about her daughter; she must have said that I forbid her to see her, to come up to my home.

AMALIA: No! She was full of regard and kindness for you!

DINA: She spoke nothing but good of you!

AGAZZI: And she said that she herself refrains from going up to her daughter's home out of respect for a feeling of yours, which, we tell you frankly, we don't understand.

MRS. SIRELLI: In fact, if we had to say exactly what we think about it . . .

AGAZZI: Yes, it seemed to us like an act of cruelty, that's what! Real cruelty!

PONZA: I am here precisely to clarify that, Your Honor. This woman's condition is most pitiable. But mine is no less pitiable, when you add the fact that it obliges me to make apologies, to give you an accounting and an explanation for a misfortune that only . . . that only such duress as this could compel me to reveal. (*He stops for a moment to look at everybody, then says slowly and articulately:*) Mrs. Frola is insane.

ALL (*with a start*): Insane?

PONZA: For four years now.

MRS. SIRELLI (*in an outcry*): Oh, God, but she doesn't seem to be at all!

AGAZZI (*dazed*): What do you mean, insane?

PONZA: She doesn't seem to be, but she *is* insane. And her madness takes the very form of believing that I won't allow her to see her daughter. (*In a frenzy of terrible, almost savage, agitation:*) What daughter, in God's name, since her daughter died four years ago?

ALL (*astonished*): Died?—Oh!—How's that?—Died?

PONZA: Four years ago. And she went mad for that very reason.

SIRELLI: But then, the lady who lives with you?—

PONZA: I married her two years ago: she's my second wife.

AMALIA: And Mrs. Frola thinks that it's still her daughter?

PONZA: That was her good luck, if you can say that. She saw me walking in the street with my second wife, from the window of the room where they kept her under guard; she thought she saw her daughter again, alive, in her; and she began to laugh, and to shake all over; she roused herself all at once from the gloomy lethargy she had fallen into, and emerged into this new madness, at first exultant and blissful, then gradually calmer, but anguished—into a resigned state that she herself submitted to; and nevertheless contented, as you could see. She stubbornly goes on believing that her daughter isn't really dead, but that I want to keep her all to myself, without letting her see her any more. She's cured, in a way. So much so that, to hear her speak, you would no longer think her insane at all.

AMALIA: Not at all! Not at all!

MRS. SIRELLI: Yes, she said specifically that she's contented with the way things are.

PONZA: She says that to everybody. And she is sincerely affectionate and grateful to me. Because I try to confirm her belief as much as I can, even at the cost of great sacrifices. I have to maintain two households. I compel my wife—who fortunately obliges me out of a feeling of charity—to humor her continually in her delusion, by pretending to be her daughter. She appears at the window, talks to her, writes to her. But charity and duty can only go so far, ladies and gentlemen! I cannot force my wife to share our home with her. And meanwhile the poor woman is practically imprisoned, locked up, for fear that *she* should come into her home. Yes, she's calm and of such a gentle nature; but you must understand, my wife would shudder from head to foot if she were ever caressed by her.

AMALIA   (*in an outburst of mingled horror and pity*): Certainly, the poor woman, just imagine!

MRS. SIRELLI   (*to her husband and Mrs. Cini*): Oh, so she herself— you hear?—wants to be locked in!

PONZA   (*to cut things short*): Your Honor, you will understand that I could not allow her to make this call if I weren't forced to.

AGAZZI: Oh, I understand, I understand now; yes, yes, it's all clear to me.

PONZA: A man with a misfortune such as mine has to keep apart. Since I was compelled to let my mother-in-law come here, it was my duty to make this declaration to you: that is, out of respect for the position I hold; because a public servant should not be suspected by the citizenry of such monstrous behavior: that, out of jealousy or some other reason, I prevent a poor mother from seeing her daughter. (*He rises.*) Your Honor! (*He bows; then, nodding his head to Laudisi and Sirelli:*) Gentlemen. (*He exits through the principal door.*)

AMALIA   (*dumbfounded*): Ooh . . . so she's crazy!

MRS. SIRELLI: Poor woman! Crazy.

DINA: That's why! She thinks she's the mother, and that other woman isn't her daughter! (*She hides her face in her hands in horror.*) My God!

MRS. CINI: But who would ever have imagined it?

AGAZZI: And yet . . . Ha! From the way she was speaking—

LAUDISI: You had already caught on?

AGAZZI: No . . . but certainly . . . she herself couldn't tell her story straight!

MRS. SIRELLI: Naturally, the poor thing: her mind doesn't work!

SIRELLI: But, on the other hand, it's peculiar, for a madwoman! Her mind wasn't clear, certainly. But the way she tried to explain why her son-in-law wouldn't allow her to see her daughter; making excuses for him, and following up the excuses she had just invented . . .

AGAZZI: Oh, fine! That's the very proof that she's crazy! That attempt to find excuses for her son-in-law, and never managing to find one that would hold water.

AMALIA: Yes! She kept contradicting herself.

AGAZZI: (*to Sirelli*): And do you think that, if she weren't crazy, she could accept these terms of seeing her daughter only at a window, with the excuse she cited, about the morbid love of a husband who wants his wife all to himself?

SIRELLI: That's just it!—as a madwoman, she accepts them? And is resigned to them? It seems odd to me, it seems odd to me. (*To Laudisi:*) What do you say about it?

LAUDISI: I? Nothing!

SCENE SIX

Butler, the foregoing, then Mrs. Frola.

BUTLER   (*knocks at the door, appears on the threshold, uneasy*): Pardon. Mrs. Frola is here again.

AMALIA   (*alarmed*): Oh, God, now? Can't we get rid of her any more?

MRS. SIRELLI: Oh, I understand: knowing that she's crazy!

MRS. CINI: My God, my God! Who knows what else she'll say now? I'd really like to hear her!

SIRELLI: I'd be curious, too. I, for one, am not at all convinced that she's crazy.

DINA: Go on, Mother! There's nothing to be frightened of: she's so calm!

AGAZZI: We'll have to receive her, certainly. Let's hear what she wants. If anything occurs, we'll take steps. But seated, seated. We must be seated. (*To the Butler:*) Show her in.

The Butler exits.

AMALIA: Help me, all of you, I beg you! I no longer know what to say to her!

Mrs. Frola enters once more. Amalia rises and goes up to her in a state of fright; the others look at her in alarm.

MRS. FROLA: May I?

AMALIA: Come in, come in, Mrs. Frola. My lady friends are still here, as you see—

MRS. FROLA   (*with extremely sad affability, smiling*): Here, and looking at me—as you are, too, my kind lady—as if at a poor mad-woman, true?

AMALIA: No, Mrs. Frola, what are you saying?

MRS. FROLA   (*with deep sorrow*): Oh, it was better when I was rude to you, Mrs. Agazzi, when I left you standing outside my door, as I did the first time! I would never have thought that you would come back and compel me to make this call, whose consequences I had unfortunately foreseen!

AMALIA: But no, believe me: we're happy to see you again.

SIRELLI: Mrs. Frola is in distress . . . we don't know why; let's let her speak.

MRS. FROLA: Didn't my son-in-law just now leave here?

AGAZZI: Oh, yes! But he came . . . he came, Mrs. Frola, to speak to me about . . . about certain office matters, that's what.

MRS. FROLA   (*hurt, dismayed*): Oh, that pious lie you're telling me to calm me down . . .

AGAZZI: No, no, Mrs. Frola, rest assured; I'm telling you the truth.

MRS. FROLA   (*as above*): Was he calm, at least? Did he speak calmly?

AGAZZI: Yes, yes, calmly, extremely calmly, right?

Everyone expresses agreement and confirmation.

MRS. FROLA: Oh, God, ladies and gentlemen, you think you are reas-suring me, while, on the other hand, I want to reassure *you* on *his* account!

MRS. SIRELLI: About what, Mrs. Frola? We tell you again that—

AGAZZI: He spoke to me about office matters . . .

MRS. FROLA: But I see how you're looking at me! Be patient. It's not for my sake! From the way you're looking at me, I can tell that he came here and gave you proof of something I would never have revealed for all the money in the world! You're all my witnesses that, a little while ago here, I didn't know how to reply to your questions, which—take my word for it—were very cruel ones for me; and I gave you an explanation of our way of life that can't satisfy anyone, I realize it! But could I tell you the real reason? Or could I say to you, as *he* goes around saying, that my daughter died four years ago and that I am a poor madwoman who thinks she's still alive and that he won't let me see her?

AGAZZI   (*dazed by the tone of enormous sincerity in which Mrs. Frola has spoken*): Ah . . . how's that? Your daughter?

MRS. FROLA   (*quickly, anxiously*): Do you see that it's true? Why do you want to hide it from me? He told you all that . . .

SIRELLI   (*hesitantly, but studying her*): Yes . . . in fact . . . he said . . .

MRS. FROLA: I know! And unfortunately I know how upset he gets when he finds himself forced to say that about me! It's a misfortune, Your Honor, which, at the cost of many efforts and a lot of pain, we've been able to overcome; but only on the condition of living the way we live. Yes, I understand that it must attract attention and arouse gossip and suspicions. But, on the other hand, he is an excellent employee, zealous, careful. You must surely have found that to be the case already.

AGAZZI: No, to tell the truth, I haven't had occasion yet to do so.

MRS. FROLA: For mercy's sake, don't judge him by his appearance! He is a fine worker; all his superiors have said so. And why must he now be tortured by this investigation into his private life, into his misfortune, which, I repeat, he has already gotten over, and which, if made public, could injure his career?

AGAZZI: No, no, Mrs. Frola, don't upset yourself like this! Nobody wants to torture him.

MRS. FROLA: My God, how am I not to get upset when I see him forced to give everybody an explanation that's—absurd! And, in fact, horrible! Can all of you seriously believe that my daughter is dead? That I am insane? That the lady he has with him is a second wife?—It's a necessity, believe me, it's a necessity for him to say that! Only on that condition was it possible to restore his peace of mind, his self-confidence. And yet he himself is aware of the monstrous nature of what he says, and, when he's forced to say it, he gets excited, he loses control: you must have seen it!

AGAZZI: Yes, in fact, he was . . . he was a little excited.

MRS. SIRELLI: Oh, my, how's that? Then, *he's* the one?

SIRELLI: Yes, it must be him! (*Triumphantly:*) I said so, everybody!

AGAZZI: Really? Is it possible?

All the others are intensely agitated.

MRS. FROLA   (*quickly, joining her hands*): No, for mercy's sake, ladies and gentlemen! What are you thinking? That is his one sore spot that mustn't be touched! Listen, would I leave my daughter alone with him if he were really insane? No! And then you can prove it to yourself in the office, Your Honor, where he carries out all his duties in the most efficient way.

AGAZZI: Ah, but, Mrs. Frola, you have to explain to us how things stand, and clearly! Is it possible that your son-in-law came here to tell us a cock-and-bull story?

MRS. FROLA: All right, I'll explain everything to you! But he must be pitied, Your Honor!

AGAZZI: What? It's not true that your daughter is dead?

MRS. FROLA   (*horrified*): Oh, no! God forbid!

AGAZZI   (*extremely irritated, shouting*): Then *he's* the lunatic!

MRS. FROLA   (*beseechingly*): No, no . . . look . . .

SIRELLI   (*triumphantly*): Yes, yes, by God, it must be him!

MRS. FROLA: No! Look! Look! He's not insane, he's not! Let me speak!—You've seen him: he's so intense, violent . . . when he got married, he was seized with a real frenzy of love. He was almost in danger of doing physical harm to my daughter, who was rather delicate. On the advice of the physicians and of all our relatives, even his (who are no longer with us, God rest their souls!), we had to take his wife away from him secretly and put her into a nursing home. And then he—already a little affected, naturally, by that . . . excessive love of his—not finding her at home any more—oh, ladies, he fell into a furious despair; he really believed that his wife was dead; he wouldn't listen to reason; he insisted on wearing black; he did all sorts of odd things; and there was no longer any way of making him change his mind. So much so that, when (barely a year later) my daughter had regained her health and her bloom, and was brought into his presence again, he said no, it wasn't her any more; no, no; he would look at her—it wasn't her any more. Oh, ladies, what torment! He went up to her, he seemed to recognize her, and then again: no, no . . . And to make him take her back, with the aid of our friends, we had to simulate a second wedding.

MRS. SIRELLI: Oh, so that's why he says . . .

MRS. FROLA: Yes, but surely, for some time now, even he no longer believes it! He feels the need to explain it that way to other people: he can't help it! In order to feel secure, you understand? Because, from time to time, maybe, he still has a flash of fear that his dear wife might be taken away from him again. (*Quietly, with a smile of confidentiality:*) That's why he keeps her locked up—all to himself. But he worships her! I'm sure of it. And my daughter is contented. (*She rises.*) I must run along now, because I wouldn't want him to come back to my place suddenly, since he's so excited. (*Sighing softly, shaking her joined hands:*) We must be patient! That poor girl has to pretend to be not herself, but some other woman; and I . . . oh, I, must pretend to be insane, ladies and gentlemen! But what are we to do? As long as he remains calm! Don't go to any trouble, please, I know the way. Good-bye, ladies and gentlemen, good-bye.

Taking leave and bowing, she exits hurriedly, through the principal door. All remain standing, dumbfounded, thunderstruck, looking at one another. Silence.

LAUDISI   (*coming into their midst*): You're all looking at one another? Well! The truth? (*He breaks out into loud laughter:*) Ha! Ha! Ha! Ha!

CURTAIN

ACT TWO

Study in Councilman Agazzi's home. Antique furniture; old paintings on the walls; door in the back wall, with a curtain; side door stage left, leading into the living room, also with a curtain; stage right, a large fireplace, on the mantel of which a big mirror leans; on the desk, a telephone; also, a small couch, armchairs, chairs, etc.

SCENE ONE

Agazzi, Laudisi, Sirelli.

Agazzi is standing near the desk, with the telephone receiver to his ear. Laudisi and Sirelli, seated, are looking in his direction, expectantly.

AGAZZI: Hello?—Yes.—Is this Centuri speaking?—Well?—Yes, good! (*He listens for a while, then:*) What? Excuse me! Is it possible? (*He listens for another while, then:*) I understand, but if you put a little effort into it . . . (*Another long pause, then:*) Excuse me, but it's really strange that you can't . . . (*Pause.*) I understand, yes . . . I understand. (*Pause.*) That's enough. Look into it . . . Good-bye. (*He puts back the receiver and steps forward.*)

SIRELLI   (*anxiously*): Well?

AGAZZI: Nothing.

SIRELLI: They can't find anything?

AGAZZI: Everything is dispersed or destroyed: town hall, archives, registry.

SIRELLI: But the testimony of some survivor?

25

AGAZZI: There's no report of survivors; and if there *are* any, by this
          time it would be highly difficult to trace them!

SIRELLI: So, then, we have no recourse but to believe one or the other
          of them, just like that, with no proof?

AGAZZI: Unfortunately!

LAUDISI: (*rising*): Want to follow my advice? Believe both of them.

AGAZZI: How can we possibly—

SIRELLI: If one says white and the other says black?

LAUDISI: Well, then, don't believe either of them!

SIRELLI: You're joking. We have no proofs, no solid facts; but, by God,
          the truth must be on one side or the other!

LAUDISI: Facts! Yes, indeed! What would you want to gather from
          them?

AGAZZI: Come now! The death certificate of the daughter, for exam-
          ple, if Mrs. Frola is the crazy one (unfortunately it can't be
          found now, because nothing can be found now), but it had to
          exist; it might turn up tomorrow; and then—once that docu-
          ment is found—it's clear that he, the son-in-law, would be
          right.

SIRELLI: Could you deny the incontrovertible truth, if someone
          showed you that document tomorrow?

LAUDISI: I? But I don't deny a thing! Far from it! You are the ones, not
          me, who need solid facts and records in order to confirm or
          deny! I have no use for them, because for me the reality does-
          n't dwell in them, but in the minds of those two people,
          which I can't conceivably enter into, except to the extent that
          they tell me about it.

SIRELLI: Fine! And don't they tell you precisely that one of the two is
          crazy? Either she is crazy or he is crazy: there's no getting
          away from that! Which one of the two?

AGAZZI: That's the question!

LAUDISI: First of all, it's not true that both of them say that. He, Mr.
          Ponza, says it about his mother-in-law. Mrs. Frola denies it,
          not only about herself, but also about him. If anything, she
          says that he was a little unsettled in his mind by an excess of
          love. But that now he's sane, as sane as can be.

SIRELLI: Ah, so, like me, you lean toward what she, the mother-in-law,
          says?

AGAZZI: Certainly, if you accept what she says, everything can be ex-
          plained very well.

LAUDISI: But everything can be equally well explained if you accept what he, the son-in-law, says!

SIRELLI: So, then, neither of the two is crazy? But one of them must be, by God!

LAUDISI: Then, which one? The two of you can't say, just as nobody can say. And it's not because those solid facts you're looking for have been obliterated—dispersed or destroyed—by any kind of disaster—a fire, an earthquake—no—but because *they* have obliterated them within themselves, in their own minds—will you try to understand?—she creating for him, or he for her, a fantasy that has the same consistency as reality, and in which they now live in perfect harmony, pacified. And this reality of theirs can't be destroyed by any document because they live and breathe inside it, they see it, they hear it, they touch it!—At the most, the document could be useful to you, to relieve you of your foolish curiosity. You haven't got it, and there you are, condemned to the astonishing torture of having in front of you, alongside you, the fantasy on one side and the reality on the other, and not being able to tell them apart!

AGAZZI: You're philosophizing, my good fellow, philosophizing! We'll see, we'll see now if it isn't possible!

SIRELLI: First we heard one of them; then, the other. Now, if we bring them together face to face, don't you think we'll discover where the fantasy, and where the reality, lies?

LAUDISI: I ask your permission to go on laughing up to the end.

AGAZZI: Good, good; we'll see who finally laughs best. Let's not waste time! (*He goes to the door at stage left and calls:*) Amalia, Mrs. Sirelli, come in, come here!

SCENE TWO

Amalia, Mrs. Sirelli, Dina, the foregoing.

MRS. SIRELLI   (*to Laudisi, wagging a finger at him*): Still? You, still?

SIRELLI: He's incorrigible!

MRS. SIRELLI: How is it you aren't infected by the frenzy that we all feel now, to get to the heart of this mystery, which is likely to drive us all crazy? *I* didn't sleep a wink last night!

AGAZZI: Please, Mrs. Sirelli, give him up!

LAUDISI: Instead, pay attention to my brother-in-law, who is arranging for a good night's sleep tonight.

AGAZZI: All right, then. Let's set this up. Good! You ladies will call on Mrs. Frola . . .

AMALIA: But will we be received?

AGAZZI: Oh, yes, I think so!

DINA: It's our duty to return her call.

AMALIA: But if he won't allow her to make or receive any?

SIRELLI: That was before!—because nobody knew anything yet. But now that she has spoken, under constraint, explaining in her fashion the reason for her reserve—

MRS. SIRELLI (*continuing*): Maybe, instead, she'll enjoy telling us about her daughter.

DINA: She's so agreeable! Oh, I tell you, there's no doubt in *my* mind: *he's* the crazy one!

AGAZZI: Let's not be too hasty, let's not be too hasty to judge.—All right, hear me out. (*He looks at the clock:*) You'll stay there just a little while; not more than fifteen minutes.

SIRELLI (*to his wife*): For goodness' sake, pay attention!

MRS. SIRELLI (*flying into a rage*): Why do you say that to *me?*

SIRELLI: Because, once you start in talking . . .

DINA (*to prevent an argument between them*): Fifteen minutes, fifteen minutes; *I'll* watch the time.

AGAZZI: I will go to the Governor's office, and I'll be back here at eleven. In about twenty minutes.

SIRELLI (*wildly impatient*): And me?

AGAZZI: Wait a minute. (*To the women:*) On some pretext, a little before that, you will induce Mrs. Frola to come here.

AMALIA: And what . . . what pretext?

AGAZZI: Any pretext! You'll find one as you're talking . . . Are you so short of them? You're not women for nothing! There's Dina, there's Mrs. Sirelli . . . Naturally, you'll go into the living room. (*He goes to the door at stage left and opens it wide, drawing aside the curtain.*) This door has to stay like this—wide open—like this! so that you can be heard talking in here.—I am leaving these papers on the desk, though I'm supposed to take them with me. It's some office business prepared especially for Mr. Ponza. I will pretend to have forgotten it, and that will be my excuse for bringing him here. Then . . .

SIRELLI   (*as above*): But, excuse me, me—when am *I* supposed to come in?

AGAZZI: A few minutes after eleven—when the ladies are already in the living room, and I am here with him. You come to pick up your wife. You have yourself shown into this room, to see me. Then I will invite all the ladies to grace us with their presence—

LAUDISI   (*quickly*): And the truth will be discovered!

DINA: Come now, Uncle—when the two of them are face to face . . .

AGAZZI: For God's sake, pay no attention to him. Run along, run along. There's no time to waste!

MRS. SIRELLI: Let's go, yes, let's go. (*To Laudisi:*) I'm not even going to say good-bye to *you!*

LAUDISI: In that case, I say good-bye to myself in your name. (*He does a handshake with his own two hands.*) Good luck!

Amalia, Dina and Mrs. Sirelli exit.

AGAZZI   (*to Sirelli*): We ought to be going, too. And right away.

SIRELLI: Yes, let's go. Good-bye, Lamberto.

LAUDISI: Good-bye, good-bye.

Agazzi and Sirelli exit.

SCENE THREE

Laudisi alone, then the Butler.

LAUDISI   (*walks around the study for a while, grinning sarcastically to himself and shaking his head; then he stops in front of the big mirror on the mantelpiece, looks at his own image and says to it:*) Oh, here you are! (*He greets it with two fingers, winking one eye slyly, and sneers:*) Well, my dear fellow!—Which of us two is the crazy one? (*He raises one hand with the index finger pointing to his image, which simultaneously points its fin-*

ger at him. He sneers again, then says:) Oh, I know: I say it's
you, and you point to me with your finger.—Go on, we two
know each other well, and intimately.—The trouble is that
the others don't see you as I see you! And then, my dear fellow, what becomes of you? I tell myself that, here in front of
you, I see and touch myself; what then becomes of you, according to how the others see you? You become an illusion,
my friend, an illusion!—Well, do you see these madmen?
Without noticing the illusion they carry along with them,
within themselves, in their wild curiosity they chase after
other people's illusions! And they think it's something totally
different.

*The Butler, who has entered, is dumbfounded on hearing Laudisi's last
words spoken into the mirror. Then he calls out:*

BUTLER: Mr. Laudisi!
LAUDISI: Yes?
BUTLER: Two ladies are here. Mrs. Cini and another.
LAUDISI: They want *me?*
BUTLER: They asked for Mrs. Agazzi. I said she was paying a call on
Mrs. Frola next door, and then . . .
LAUDISI: Then?
BUTLER: They looked at each other; then they tapped their hands
with their gloves—"Oh, really? Oh, really?"—and, eager as
can be, they asked me if no one was here at all.
LAUDISI: You surely said no one was here.
BUTLER: I replied that *you* were here.
LAUDISI: I—no. If anyone, it's the man that *they* know.
BUTLER (*more dumbfounded than ever*): How's that?
LAUDISI: Do you really think it's the same thing?
BUTLER (*as above, cheerlessly attempting a smile with his mouth
open*): I don't understand.
LAUDISI: With whom are you speaking right now?
BUTLER (*overcome*): What do you mean . . . with whom am I speak-
ing . . . With *you* . . .
LAUDISI: And are you completely sure that I'm the same man those
ladies are asking for?
BUTLER: But . . . I don't know . . . They said Mrs. Agazzi's brother . . .
LAUDISI: Fine! Ah . . . Yes, in that case, it's me, it's me . . . Show them
in, show them in . . .

*The Butler exits, turning around a few times to look at him as if he no
longer believed his eyes.*

SCENE FOUR

Laudisi, Mrs. Cini, Mrs. Nenni.

MRS. CINI: May we?

LAUDISI: Come in, come in, ma'am.

MRS. CINI: They told me Mrs. Agazzi was out. I had brought my
friend Mrs. Nenni with me (*she indicates her, an old woman
even more foolish and mincing than herself, equally full of
morbid curiosity, but cautious and timid*); she wished so to
meet Mrs.—

LAUDISI (*quickly*): Frola?

MRS. CINI: No, no: your sister!

LAUDISI: Oh, she'll come, she'll be here before long. So will Mrs.
Frola. Please take a seat. (*He invites them to sit on the small
couch; then, neatly sitting down between them:*) May I? All
three of us can sit here comfortably. Mrs. Sirelli is also at Mrs.
Frola's.

MRS. CINI: Yes, the butler told us so.

LAUDISI: All orchestrated, you know! Oh, it's going to be a great scene,
one to remember! Very soon, at eleven. Here.

MRS.CINI (*dazed*): Pardon me, what is orchestrated?

LAUDISI (*mysteriously; first making the gesture of bringing his two
index fingers together; then saying*): The meeting. (*He makes
a gesture of admiration, then says:*) A monumental idea!

MRS. CINI: What . . . what meeting?

LAUDISI: Of the two of them. First, *he'll* come into *this* room.

MRS. CINI: Mr. Ponza?

LAUDISI: Yes; and *she'll* be led into *that* one. (*He points to the living
room.*)

MRS. CINI: Mrs. Frola?

LAUDISI: Yes, ma'am. (*Again, first making an expressive hand gesture,
then saying:*) But after that, both of them in here, face to face

with each other; and us, all around, watching and listening.
A monumental idea!

MRS. CINI: In order to find out—?

LAUDISI: The truth! But we know it already. All that remains now is to
unmask it.

MRS. CINI   (*surprised and extremely nervous*): Oh! You found out?
Which one is it? Which of the two? Who is it?

LAUDISI: Let's see . . . Guess. Who do you say it is?

MRS. CINI   (*delighted, hesitantly*): But . . . I . . . Now . . .

LAUDISI: Her or him? Let's see . . . Guess . . . Come on!

MRS. CINI: I . . . I say him!

LAUDISI   (*after looking at her for a moment*): It *is* him.

MRS. CINI   (*delighted*): Yes! Ah! There you go! Of course! It had to be
him, it had to!

MRS. NENNI   (*delighted*): Him!—Well, we women said that all along!

MRS. CINI: And how, how did you come to find out? Proofs turned
up, right? Documents.

MRS. NENNI: Through the police department, right? We said so! It
was impossible that they couldn't find out through the
Governor's office!

LAUDISI   (*signals to them with his hands to draw closer to him; then,
quietly, with a mysterious air, as if weighing each syllable*):
The certificate of the second marriage.

MRS. CINI   (*as if receiving a slap in the face*): The second?

MRS. NENNI   (*confused*): What? What? The second marriage?

MRS. CINI   (*recovering, vexed*): But then . . . then *he* would be right?

LAUDISI: Ah! The solid facts, ladies! The certificate of the second marriage—so it would seem—speaks clearly.

MRS. NENNI   (*close to tears*): But then *she* is the crazy one!

LAUDISI: Right. So it would seem.

MRS. CINI: But how is that? First you said him and now you say her?

LAUDISI: Yes, ma'am. Because the certificate, this certificate of the
second marriage, may very well be what Mrs. Frola assured us
it was—a simulated certificate, do you follow me?—created
as a ruse, with the help of their friends, to humor his fixation
that his wife was no longer the same woman, but someone
else.

MRS. CINI: Oh, but then the certificate . . . would be just worthless?

LAUDISI: That depends, ladies . . . It would have the value that each
person wanted to place on it! Listen, aren't there also the

notes Mrs. Frola says she receives from her daughter every day by way of the basket, in the courtyard there? Those notes exist, don't they?

MRS. CINI: Yes; and so?

LAUDISI: Well: they're documents, ma'am! Those notes are documents, too! But all according to the value *she* is willing to place on them! Mr. Ponza comes along and says they're a fake, created to humor Mrs. Frola's fixation.

MRS. CINI: My God, but then nothing is known for certain!

LAUDISI: Why nothing? Why nothing? Let's not exaggerate! Tell me, how many days are there in a week?

MRS. CINI: Why, seven.

LAUDISI: Monday, Tuesday, Wednesday . . .

MRS. CINI   (*who follows his prompting to continue*): Thursday, Friday, Saturday . . .

LAUDISI: And Sunday! (*Turning to the other woman:*) And the months of the year?

MRS. NENNI: Twelve!

LAUDISI: January, February, March . . .

MRS. CINI: We get it! You're making fun of us!

SCENE FIVE

The foregoing. Dina.

DINA   (*running in from the back door*): Uncle, please . . . (*She stops, seeing Mrs. Cini:*) Oh, Mrs. Cini, you're here?

MRS. CINI: Yes, I came with Mrs. Nenni—

LAUDISI: Who wishes so to meet Mrs. Frola.

MRS. NENNI: No, no, excuse me . . .

MRS. CINI: He's still laughing at us! Oh, dear Miss Agazzi! He shook us up totally! It's like arriving at a railroad station—bam! bam!—and being endlessly switched from one track to another! We're dizzy!

DINA: Oh! He's been so mean recently, to all of us! Be patient. I no longer need anything. I'll go tell Mother that you're here: that will be enough.—Oh, Uncle, if you had only heard her, what

a darling old lady! How she speaks! Such kindness!—And
what a neat home, everything orderly; everything in good
taste; white cloths on the furniture . . . She showed us all her
daughter's notes.

MRS. CINI: Yes . . . but . . . if, as Mr. Laudisi was just telling us . . .

DINA: What does *he* know about them? He hasn't read them!

MRS. NENNI: Couldn't they be a fake?

DINA: What do you mean, fake? Pay no attention to him! Could a
mother ever be mistaken about how her own daughter expresses herself? The latest note, yesterday's . . . (*She stops
short, hearing the sound of voices from the adjacent living
room through the door that has been left open:*) Ah, here they
are: they're already here, I'm sure! (*She goes to the living-room
door to look.*)

MRS. CINI   (*running after her*): With *her*? With Mrs. Frola?

DINA: Yes. Let them come, let them come. We all have to be in the
living room. Is it eleven yet, Uncle?

SCENE SIX

The foregoing, Amalia.

AMALIA   (*arriving, but through the living-room door; she, too, is agitated*): We can do without it now! There's no more need for
proofs.

DINA: You're right! I think so, too! By this time it's pointless!

AMALIA   (*hastily greeting Mrs. Cini, sadly and anxiously*): My dear
Mrs. Cini.

MRS. CINI   (*introducing Mrs. Nenni*): Mrs. Nenni, who has come with
me to . . .

AMALIA   (*hastily greeting Mrs. Nenni, too*): A pleasure, Mrs. Nenni.
(*Then:*) There's no longer any doubt! It's him!

MRS. CINI: It's him, isn't it? It's him?

DINA: If we could only forewarn Father, so we wouldn't have to go on
playing this trick on that poor lady!

AMALIA: Yes! We've brought her into the next room! I feel just as if I
were betraying her!

LAUDISI: Yes! It's shameful, shameful. You're both right! All the more
so since it's beginning to appear evident to me that it must be
her! Her, surely!

AMALIA: Her? What? What are you saying?

LAUDISI: Her, her, her.

AMALIA: Oh, go away!

DINA: *We* are almost certain of the opposite by now!

MRS. CINI AND MRS. NENNI (*delighted*): Yes? Oh, yes?

LAUDISI: And precisely because *you* are so sure about it!

DINA: Let's leave, let's go in there; can't you see he's doing it on purpose?

AMALIA: Let's go, yes, let's go, ladies. (*In front of the door at stage left:*)
After you.

Mrs. Cini, Mrs. Nenni and Amalia exit. Dina begins to exit also.

LAUDISI   (*calling her over*): Dina!

DINA: I don't want to listen to you! No! No!

LAUDISI: Close that door again if you now find the proof unnecessary.

DINA: And Father? He's the one who left it open like this. He'll soon
be here with that man. If he found it closed . . . You know
how Father is!

LAUDISI: But you will all convince him (especially you, Dina) that there
was no longer any need to keep it open. Aren't you convinced?

DINA: Thoroughly!

LAUDISI   (*with a smile of challenge*): Then close it!

DINA: You'd like to have the pleasure of watching me hesitate some
more. I won't close it. But just for Father's sake.

LAUDISI   (*as above*): Would you like *me* to close it?

DINA: On your own responsibility!

LAUDISI: But I don't have the same certainty you do that *he* is the
crazy one.

DINA: Well, come into the living room, listen to Mrs. Frola talk the
way *we* heard her, and you'll see that you won't have any
doubts left, either.

LAUDISI: Yes, I'm coming. And it's really all right for me to close the
door. On my own responsibility.

DINA: There, you see? Even before you've heard her talk!

LAUDISI: No, dear. Because I'm sure that by this time your father also
thinks, just as you ladies do, that this experiment is needless.

DINA: You're sure of that?

LAUDISI: Of course! He's now talking to *him!* Without a doubt he has

become convinced that *she* is the crazy one. (*He approaches
the door resolutely.*) I'll shut it.

DINA   (*suddenly restraining him*): No. (*Then, regaining self-control:*)
Excuse me . . . if that's what you think . . . let's leave it open . . .

LAUDISI   (*laughing in his manner*): Ha! Ha! Ha!

DINA: I mean, for Father's sake!

LAUDISI: And your father will say for your sake!—Let's leave it open.

*The piano is heard from the adjacent living room; someone is playing an
old aria, full of sweet, sad grace, from Paisiello's opera* Nina pazza per
amore [Nina Driven Mad by Love].

DINA: Oh, it's her . . . do you hear? She's playing! *She's* playing!

LAUDISI: The old lady?

DINA: Yes, she told us that her daughter always used to play that old
aria. Do you hear how sweetly she plays it? Let's go, let's go.

They both exit through the door at stage left.

SCENE SEVEN

Agazzi, Mr. Ponza, then Sirelli.

*After Laudisi and Dina exit, the stage remains empty for a while. The
piano is still heard from inside. Mr. Ponza, entering through the back
door with Councilman Agazzi, is deeply disturbed on hearing that music,
and his distress increases gradually in the course of the scene.*

AGAZZI   (*behind the back door*): After you, after you. (*He ushers in Mr.
Ponza, then enters himself and heads for the desk to pick up the
papers he pretends to have forgotten there.*) There, I must have
left them here. Have a seat, please. (*Mr. Ponza remains standing, agitatedly looking in the direction of the living room,
where the sound of the piano is coming from.*) Yes, here they
are! (*He takes the papers and approaches Mr. Ponza, leafing
through them.*) As I was telling you, it's an entangled dispute
that's been dragging on for years. (*He, too, turns and looks in
the direction of the living room, annoyed by the sound of the
piano.*) That music! Now of all times! (*He makes a gesture of

vexation as he turns, as if saying to himself, "Those stupid women!") Who's playing? (*He goes to look into the living room through the door; seeing Mrs. Frola at the piano, he acts surprised:*) Oh! What do you know!

PONZA   (*approaching him, livid*): In God's name, is it her? Is it her that's playing?

AGAZZI: Yes, your mother-in-law! And how well she plays!

PONZA: But how come? Did they bring her here again? And are they making her play?

AGAZZI: I don't see what harm there can be in it!

PONZA: No, no, for heaven's sake! Not that music! It's what her daughter used to play!

AGAZZI: Oh, perhaps it hurts you to hear her play it?

PONZA: Not *me*! It hurts *her*! And it hurts her enormously! And yet I told you and the ladies, Your Honor, the circumstances of that poor, unhappy woman—

AGAZZI   (*trying to calm his ever-increasing agitation*): Yes, yes, but look—

PONZA   (*continuing*): I told you she needs to be left in peace! That she mustn't receive calls or make any! I'm the only one, the only one, who knows how to handle her! They're destroying her, destroying her!

AGAZZI: No, no, why do you say that? My ladies must surely also be able to . . . (*He stops short as the music ends in the living room, from which a chorus of praise now issues:*) There, take a look . . . you can hear . . .

From inside can be distinctly heard the following lines of dialogue:

DINA: But you still play excellently, Mrs. Frola!

MRS. FROLA: I? Ah, my Lina! You should hear how my Lina plays it!

PONZA   (*furious, wringing his hands*): Her Lina! You hear? She says her Lina!

AGAZZI: Yes, her daughter.

PONZA: But she says "plays"! she says "plays"!

Again, from inside, distinctly:

MRS. FROLA: Ah, no, she can no longer play, since *that time!* And perhaps that's her greatest sorrow, poor girl!

AGAZZI: It seems natural to me . . . She thinks she's still alive . . .

PONZA: But she mustn't be allowed to talk that way! She mustn't . . .

she mustn't say that . . . Did you hear? "Since *that time*" . . .
She said "since *that time*"! On *that* piano, of course! You
don't know! On that poor dead girl's piano!

*At this moment they are joined by Sirelli, who, hearing Ponza's last few
words and noticing his extreme agitation, remains thunderstruck. Agazzi,
himself alarmed, signals to him to approach.*

AGAZZI: I beg of you, have the ladies come in!

*Sirelli, keeping at a distance, heads for the door at stage left and calls the
ladies.*

PONZA: The ladies? In here? No, no! Rather than that . . .

SCENE EIGHT

Mrs. Frola, Amalia, Mrs. Sirelli, Dina, Mrs. Cini,
Mrs. Nenni, Laudisi, the foregoing.

*The ladies, heeding the call of Sirelli, who was obviously dismayed, enter
in alarm. Mrs. Frola, catching sight of her son-in-law in that state of
frenzy, almost a bestial rage, is frightened. In the scene that follows, as-
saulted by him with extreme violence, she from time to time makes knowing signs to the others with her eyes. The scene is to be played swiftly and
excitedly.*

PONZA: You here? Here again? What did you come for?
MRS. FROLA: Be patient! I came . . .
PONZA: You came here to tell them again . . . What *did* you tell them?
What did you tell these ladies?
MRS. FROLA: Nothing, I swear to you! Nothing!
PONZA: Nothing? How can you say it was nothing? I heard! This gen-
tleman (*pointing to Agazzi*) heard it, too! You said "she plays"!
Who plays? Lina plays? You know very well that your daugh-
ter died four years ago!
MRS. FROLA: Of course, dear! Calm yourself! Yes, yes!
PONZA: "And she can no longer play, since *that time!*" Naturally, she
can't play any longer *since that time!* How do you want her to
play if she's dead?

MRS. FROLA: Of course! Certainly! Didn't I say so, ladies? I said she can't any longer, since that time—seeing that she's dead!

PONZA: Then, why are you still thinking about that piano?

MRS. FROLA: I? No, I no longer think about it! I no longer think about it!

PONZA: *I* demolished it! And you know that! When your daughter died! So that the other woman wouldn't play—and anyway, she doesn't know how to play. You know that this other woman *doesn't play* the piano.

MRS. FROLA: Of course! She doesn't know how!

PONZA: And what was your daughter's name? Her name was Lina, right? Now tell us my second wife's name! Tell everybody here, because you know it very well!—What's her name?

MRS. FROLA: Giulia! Her name is Giulia! Yes, yes, that's the whole truth, ladies and gentlemen; her name is Giulia!

PONZA: Giulia, then, not Lina! And don't try to give them a wink all the time that you're saying her name is Giulia!

MRS. FROLA: I? No! I didn't wink!

PONZA: I saw you! You winked! I got a good look! You want to ruin me! You'd have these people believe I still want to keep your daughter all to myself—as if she weren't dead. (*Breaks out into terrible sobbing.*) As if she weren't dead!

MRS. FROLA   (*quickly, with enormous tenderness and humility, running up to him*): I? No! No, son! No, dear! Calm down, I beg you. I never said that . . . Right? Right, ladies?

AMALIA, MRS. SIRELLI, DINA: It's true! True! She never said that! She always said she was dead!

MRS. FROLA: Right? I said she was dead! Of course. And that you are so kind to me! (*To the ladies:*) Right? Right? I, ruin you? I, compromise you?

PONZA   (*drawing himself up, an awesome figure*): But meanwhile you go around looking for the piano in other people's homes, to play your daughter's little pieces, and you go around saying that Lina plays them that way, or even better!

MRS. FROLA: No, it was . . . I did it . . . only . . . only to try out . . .

PONZA: You can't! You mustn't! Where do you get the notion of continuing to play what your dead daughter used to play?

MRS. FROLA: You're right, yes, oh, you poor man . . . You poor man! (*Touched, she starts to weep.*) I won't do it again! I won't do it again!

PONZA   (*looming right over her menacingly*): Go! Go away! Go away!

Mrs. Frola: Yes . . . yes . . . I'm going, I'm going . . . Oh, God!

As she withdraws, she makes beseeching gestures to one and all to have consideration for her son-in-law, and she exits weeping.

SCENE NINE

The foregoing, except Mrs. Frola.

All remain stricken with pity and terror, looking at Mr. Ponza. But suddenly, as soon as his mother-in-law has gone, he changes, acts calmly, resumes his normal manner, and says in a simple way:

Ponza: Ladies and gentlemen, please excuse me for the unpleasant scene I had to act out, in order to remedy the harm which, without meaning to, without being aware of it, you are causing this unhappy woman with your pity.

Agazzi   (*dumbfounded like all the rest*): What? You were pretending?

Ponza: I had to, ladies and gentlemen! Don't you understand that this is the only way to humor her in her delusion?—to shout the truth at her this way, as if it were madness on my part? Forgive me and allow me to take my leave: now I must run over to her place.

He rushes off through the back door. Again, everyone is dumbfounded, silently looking at one another.

Laudisi   (*placing himself in their midst*): There you have it, ladies and gentlemen, the truth has been discovered. (*He bursts out laughing:*) Ha! Ha! Ha! Ha!

CURTAIN

ACT THREE

Same setting as Act Two.

SCENE ONE

Laudisi, Butler, Commissioner Centuri.

Laudisi is sprawling in an armchair, reading. Through the door at stage left that leads into the living room comes the confused noise of many voices. The Butler, at the back door, lets Commissioner Centuri enter.

BUTLER: This way, please. I'll let his Honor know you're here.

LAUDISI   (*turning and seeing Centuri*): Oh, Commissioner! (*He rises hurriedly and calls back the Butler, who is about to exit:*) Pst! Wait. (*To Centuri:*) Any news?

CENTURI   (*tall, stiff, gloomy, about forty*): Yes, some.

LAUDISI: Good! (*To the Butler:*) Let it go. *I'll* call my brother-in-law in here later. (*With a movement of his head he indicates the door at stage left. The Butler bows and exits.*) You've performed the miracle! A whole city is saved! Do you hear them? Do you hear how they're shouting? Well, then: any solid news?

CENTURI: About someone who could finally be traced—

LAUDISI: From Mr. Ponza's town? Townspeople with sure knowledge?

CENTURI: Yes sir. A few facts; not many, but reliable.

LAUDISI: Good, good! For example?

CENTURI: Here, I have with me the communications that were transmitted to me. (*From the inner pocket of his jacket he extracts an open yellow envelope with a sheet of paper in it, and hands it to Laudisi.*)

41

LAUDISI: Let's see, let's see! (*He removes the paper from the envelope and starts reading it silently, from time to time interjecting an "oh" or "ah" with different expressions: first, one of satisfaction; then, one of doubt; then, one resembling pity; finally, one of total disappointment.*) No! There's nothing! No certainty in this information, Commissioner!

CENTURI: It's all that could be learned.

LAUDISI: But all the doubts remain just as before! (*He looks at him; then, with a sudden resolve:*) Do you want to perform a truly good action, Commissioner? Render a meritorious service to the citizenry, one for which God will surely give you credit?

CENTURI (*looking at him in bewilderment*): What service? I don't get it!

LAUDISI: It's this. Look. Sit down there (*indicating the desk*). Tear off this half-sheet of information that says nothing at all, and here, on the other half, write some bit of information that's precise and certain.

CENTURI (*amazed*): I? How? What information?

LAUDISI: Anything at all, whatever you please! As if it were coming from these two townspeople you were able to trace.—For everyone's good! To restore peace and quiet to the whole town! They want some truth, don't they, and it doesn't matter which, as long as it's factual and categorical? Well, give it to them!

CENTURI (*forcefully, becoming heated, almost insulted*): But how am I to give it if I don't have it! Do you want me to falsify a document? I'm surprised that you dare suggest it to me! And when I say surprised, I mean something stronger! Please drop this, and do me the pleasure of announcing me to His Honor at once.

LAUDISI (*extends his arms in defeat*): At your service, immediately.

He goes to the door at stage left and opens it. Immediately the shouts of the people in the living room are heard more clearly. But the moment Laudisi crosses the threshold, the shouting stops short. And from inside is heard Laudisi's voice announcing: "Ladies and gentlemen, Commissioner Centuri is here; he brings reliable information from people who know the truth!" *The announcement is greeted with applause and shouts of "Hurray!" Commissioner Centuri is upset because he is quite aware that the news he brings is not solid enough to satisfy such a great expectation.*

SCENE TWO

Centuri, Agazzi, Sirelli, Laudisi, Amalia, Dina, Mrs. Sirelli, Mrs. Cini, Mrs. Nenni and many other ladies and gentlemen.

They all dash in through the door at stage left, Agazzi in the lead, all of them excited, exultant, clapping their hands and shouting: "Bravo, bravo, Centuri!"

AGAZZI   (*extending his hands*): Good old Centuri! I thought so all along! It was impossible that you couldn't settle the matter!

ALL: Bravo, bravo! Let's see, let's see! The proofs, at once! Which one is it? Which one is it?

CENTURI   (*amazed, bewildered, confused*): No, no . . . Your Honor, I . . .

AGAZZI: Ladies and gentlemen, please! Quiet!

CENTURI: Yes, I did all I could; but when Mr. Laudisi told you in there—

AGAZZI: That you bring us reliable news!—

SIRELLI: Precise facts!—

LAUDISI   (*loud, resolutely, forestalling Centuri*): Not many, it's true, but precise! From people who could be traced! From Mr. Ponza's town! Someone who knows the truth!

ALL: Finally! Ah, finally, finally!

CENTURI   (*shrugging his shoulders and handing the sheet to Agazzi*): Here you are, Your Honor.

AGAZZI   (*unfolding the sheet amid the throng of the others, who hastily surround him*): Ah, let's see! Let's see!

CENTURI   (*annoyed, approaching Laudisi*): But you, Mr. Laudisi . . .

LAUDISI   (*quickly, loudly*): Let him read it, please! Let him read it!

AGAZZI: A moment of patience, ladies and gentlemen! Give me room! All right, I'll read it, I'll read it!

There is a moment of silence. And then, in that silence, Laudisi's voice stands out loud and clear.

LAUDISI: *I've* already read it!

ALL   (*abandoning Agazzi and noisily rushing over to surround Laudisi*): You have? Well? What does it say? What is known?

LAUDISI   (*clearly articulating the words*): It is certain, incontrovertible, the testimony of a fellow townsman of Mr. Ponza, that Mrs. Frola has been in a nursing home!

ALL (*with regret and disappointment*): Oh!

MRS. SIRELLI: Mrs. Frola?

DINA: So it's really her?

AGAZZI (*who has read the message in the meantime, shouts, waving the sheet*): No! No! It doesn't say anything of the kind here!

ALL (*now abandoning Laudisi and rushing to surround Agazzi, shouting*): Really? What does it say? What does it say?

LAUDISI (*loud, to Agazzi*): Oh, yes! It says "the lady"! It specifically says "the lady"!

AGAZZI (*louder*): Not at all! This man says "it seems to him": he isn't at all sure of it! And, at any rate, he doesn't know whether it was the mother or the daughter!

ALL (*contentedly*): Ah!

LAUDISI (*maintaining his position*): But it must be her, the mother without a doubt!

SIRELLI: What! It's the daughter, ladies and gentlemen! The daughter!—

MRS. SIRELLI: Just as Mrs. Frola herself told us, besides!—

AMALIA: That's it! Very good! When they took her away from her husband secretly—

DINA: And shut her away in a nursing home—exactly!

AGAZZI: And, besides, this informant isn't even from the town! He says he used to go there often . . . that he doesn't remember clearly . . . that he thinks he heard this said . . .

SIRELLI: Ah! So it's just idle hearsay!

LAUDISI: Just a moment; if you're all so convinced that it's Mrs. Frola who is right, what are you still looking for? For heaven's sake, call it quits once and for all! *He's* the crazy one, and that's that!

SIRELLI: Fine, my friend! But there's the Governor who believes the opposite and conspicuously gives Mr. Ponza his full confidence!

CENTURI: Yes, it's true! The Governor believes Mr. Ponza; he said so to me, too!

AGAZZI: It's because the Governor has not yet spoken with Mrs. Frola here next door!

MRS. SIRELLI: Of course! He's spoken only with *him*!

SIRELLI: And, besides, there are others here who agree with the Governor!

A MAN: Me, me, for example, yes! Because *I* know of a similar case: a mother who went crazy over her daughter's death and believes her son-in-law won't let her see her. It's exactly the same!

SECOND MAN: No, no, in the case you mean, the son-in-law has remained unmarried and is now living alone. Whereas here, this Mr. Ponza has a woman living with him . . .

LAUDISI   (*inspired by a sudden idea*): Oh, Lord! Ladies, gentlemen! Did you hear? We've found the key to the case! Oh, Lord! Columbus' egg! (*Patting the Second Man on the shoulder:*) Bravo, bravo, my good man! Did you all hear?

ALL   (*perplexed, not understanding*): But what is it? What is it?

SECOND MAN   (*amazed*): What did I say? I don't know . . .

LAUDISI: What do you mean, what did you say? You solved the whole matter! Oh, just have a little patience, ladies and gentlemen! (*To Agazzi:*) The Governor is due to come here?

AGAZZI: Yes, we expect him . . . But why? Explain!

LAUDISI: There's no point in his coming here to speak with Mrs. Frola! Up to now he's believed the son-in-law; when he speaks with the mother-in-law, even he will no longer know which of the two to believe! No, no! In this case, the Governor needs to do something quite different. Something only he can do!

ALL: What? What?

LAUDISI   (*radiant*): What! Didn't you hear what this gentleman said? Mr. Ponza has "a woman" living with him! His wife.

SIRELLI: Make the wife talk? Yes! Yes!

DINA: But, seeing that that poor woman is kept like a prisoner?—

SIRELLI: The Governor must pull his weight and make her talk!

AMALIA: Surely she's the only one who can tell us the truth!

MRS. SIRELLI: You think so? She'll say whatever her husband wants!

LAUDISI: True! If she had to speak in his presence! Certainly.

SIRELLI: She ought to talk privately with the Governor!

AGAZZI: And the Governor could surely use his authority to make the wife confess privately how things really stand. Of course! Of course! Don't you think so, Centuri?

CENTURI: Without a doubt; if the Governor were willing!

AGAZZI: She's really the only one! He ought to be informed and spared the trouble of coming here for now. Go, you go, Centuri.

CENTURI: Yes, sir. My respects. Ladies, gentlemen. (*He bows and exits.*)

MRS. SIRELLI   (*clapping her hands*): Yes! Good for you, Laudisi!

DINA: Bravo, bravo, Uncle! What a great idea!

ALL: Bravo, bravo! Yes, she's the only one, the only one!

AGAZZI: Of course! Why didn't we think of it?

SIRELLI: It's only natural! None of us has ever seen her! It's as if she didn't exist, poor thing!

LAUDISI   (*as if struck by a new idea*): Oh! Just a minute, are you all so sure that she's there?

AMALIA: What? For heaven's sake, Lamberto!

SIRELLI   (*pretending to laugh*): Do you want to cast doubts even on her existence?

LAUDISI: Well, let's take it slowly: you yourselves say that no one has ever seen her!

DINA: Come now! There's Mrs. Frola, who sees her and talks to her every day!

MRS. SIRELLI: And he makes the same assertion, the son-in-law!

LAUDISI: Fine! But reflect for a moment. Going strictly by logic, that residence should contain nothing but a phantom.

ALL: A phantom?

AGAZZI: Come on, quit it once and for all!

LAUDISI: Let me talk.—The phantom of the second wife, if *she*, Mrs. Frola, is right. Or else the phantom of her daughter, if *he*, Mr. Ponza, is right. It now remains to be seen, ladies and gentlemen, whether this phantom in the mind of one or the other of them is a real person on her own. Having reached that point, I think that there's some justification to doubt it!

AMALIA: Go away! You want to drive all of us as crazy as you are!

MRS. NENNI: Oh, Lord, I can feel my flesh creep!

MRS. CINI: I don't know what pleasure you find in scaring us this way!

ALL: Never mind! Never mind! He's joking! He's joking!

SIRELLI: She's a flesh-and-blood woman, rest assured. And we'll make her talk! We'll make her talk!

AGAZZI: Remember, it was you who suggested we should make her talk to the Governor!

LAUDISI: Yes, it was me; *if* there really is a woman up there: I mean, any woman. But listen carefully, ladies and gentlemen: there can't be *just any* woman up there. There isn't! I, for one, now doubt that she's there.

MRS. SIRELLI: My God, you really want to drive us crazy!

LAUDISI: Well, we'll see, we'll see!

ALL   (*helter-skelter*): But she's been seen even by others!—But she looks out of the courtyard window!—She writes notes to her!—He's doing it on purpose, to make fun of us!

SCENE THREE

The foregoing; Centuri, returning.

CENTURI   (*entering in the midst of the hubbub, he himself excited, he announces*): The Governor! The Governor!

AGAZZI: What? Here? Then, what did *you* do?

CENTURI: I met him on the way, with Mr. Ponza, headed here . . .

SIRELLI: Oh, with *him*?

AGAZZI: My God, no! If he's coming with Ponza, he'll stop in at Mrs. Frola's! Please, Centuri, station yourself in front of the entrance and ask him on my behalf to be so good as to see *me* first for a moment, as he had promised.

CENTURI: Yes, sir, just as you say. I'm going. (*Exits hurriedly through the back door.*)

AGAZZI: Ladies and gentlemen, please retire into the living room for a while.

MRS. SIRELLI: But make it clear to him, please! She's the only one! The only one!

AMALIA   (*behind the door at stage left*): Come in, please, ladies.

AGAZZI: You stay, Sirelli. And you, too, Lamberto. (*All the rest, men and women, exit through the door at stage left. To Laudisi:*) Let *me* talk, please.

LAUDISI: It's all the same to me! In fact, if you want me to leave, too . . .

AGAZZI: No, no: it's better for you to stay here.—Ah, here he is.

SCENE FOUR

The foregoing, the Governor, Centuri.

GOVERNOR   (*about sixty, tall, plump, hail-fellow-well-met type*): My dear Agazzi!—Oh, you here, too, Sirelli?—My dear Laudisi. (*Shakes hands with each of them.*)

AGAZZI   (*motioning to him to sit down*): Forgive me for asking you to stop in at my place first.

GOVERNOR: I intended to all along, as I had promised. I would surely have stopped in later on.

AGAZZI   (*catching sight of Centuri still standing behind the others*): Please, Centuri, join us. Sit here.

GOVERNOR: Well, you, Sirelli—I've heard this!—are one of the people most excited and upset by this gossip about our new secretary.

SIRELLI: No, please believe me, Your Excellency, everyone in town is just as excited as I am.

AGAZZI: Yes, it's true, everyone is extremely excited.

GOVERNOR: And *I* can't see any reason for it!

AGAZZI: Because you haven't happened to be present at certain scenes, as we have, living right next to the mother-in-law.

SIRELLI: Forgive me, Your Excellency, you have not yet heard that poor lady.

GOVERNOR: It was to her place that I was just heading. (*To Agazzi:*) I had promised you I would listen to her here in your home, as you wished. But the son-in-law came to ask me, to implore me, to be so good as to go to her place (in order to put a stop to all this chatter). Do you really think he would have done so if he weren't totally sure that such a visit would furnish me with proof of his assertions?

AGAZZI: Oh, of course! Because, in his presence, that poor woman—

SIRELLI   (*picking up the thread at once*): Would say whatever he liked, Your Excellency! And that's the proof that *she's* not the crazy one!

AGAZZI: *We* made that experiment here, yesterday!

GOVERNOR: Yes, my good fellow: Precisely because he makes her believe that *he* is the crazy one! He told me about it in advance. And indeed, how otherwise could that unfortunate woman deceive herself? It's torture, believe me, torture for that poor man!

SIRELLI: Yes! *If*, on the contrary, it isn't her that's humoring *him* in his belief that her daughter is dead, so that he can rest assured that his wife won't be taken away from him again! In that case, Your Excellency, you see that the tortured one would be her, not him!

AGAZZI: That's where the doubt lies. And a similar doubt has entered your mind—

SIRELLI: Just as it has entered everybody's!—

GOVERNOR: A doubt? No; on the contrary, it seems to me there isn't even a shadow of one left in *your* minds! And, similarly, I confess to you that there's none left in mine, either, only taking the opposite view.—What about you, Laudisi?

LAUDISI: Forgive me, Your Excellency. I promised my brother-in-law not to open my mouth.

AGAZZI   (*in an outburst*): Come on, what are you talking about! If he asks you, answer!—Do you know why I told him not to talk? Because for two days now he's amused himself by muddying the waters even worse!

LAUDISI: That's not so, Your Excellency. It's just the opposite. I've done all I could to clear the waters.

SIRELLI: Sure? Do you know how? By maintaining that it's not possible to find out the truth, and, just a moment ago, by raising the suspicion that there's no woman in Mr. Ponza's home, but a phantom!

GOVERNOR   (*tickled*): What! What! That's a good one!

AGAZZI: Please! You understand: it's pointless to pay any attention to him!

LAUDISI: And yet, Your Excellency, it was at my prompting that you were invited to come here!

GOVERNOR: Because you also think it would be a good idea for me to talk to the lady next door?

LAUDISI: No, not a bit! The best thing you could do is to trust what Mr. Ponza says!

GOVERNOR: Good! Then, you also think that Mr. Ponza . . . ?

LAUDISI   (*quickly*): No. In the same way, I'd like everyone here to trust what Mrs. Frola says, and to put an end to all of this!

AGAZZI: You hear him? Does that sound like logic to you?

GOVERNOR: May I? (*To Laudisi:*) And so, in your opinion, it's also possible to lend credence to what *she* says?

LAUDISI: Absolutely! In every detail. Just as much as to what *he* says!

GOVERNOR: But, in that case? . . .

SIRELLI: But they contradict each other!

AGAZZI   (*annoyed, resolutely*): Listen to me, please! I don't lean, up to now I haven't wished to lean, toward one side or the other. *He* may be right, *she* may be right. We've got to get to the bottom of this! And there's only one way.

SIRELLI: And (*indicating Laudisi:*) he's the one who suggested it!

GOVERNOR: Really?—Well, then! Let's hear it!

AGAZZI: Since we lack every other factual proof, the only one we're left with is this: for you to use your authority and obtain the wife's confession.

GOVERNOR: Mrs. Ponza's?

SIRELLI: But, naturally, not in her husband's presence!

AGAZZI: So she can tell the truth!

SIRELLI: Whether she's Mrs. Frola's daughter, as we think it's right to believe—

AGAZZI: Or a second wife who agrees to play the daughter's part, as Mr. Ponza would have us believe—

GOVERNOR: And as *I* implicitly believe!—Yes! I agree it's the only way. Trust me, that poor chap asks for nothing better than to convince everybody he's right! He's been so obliging with me! He'll be the happiest one of all! And you will all calm down immediately, my friends.—Do me a favor, Centuri. (*Centuri rises.*) Go next door and call Mr. Ponza. Ask him on my behalf to come in here for a moment.

CENTURI: At once! (*Bows and exits through the back door.*)

AGAZZI: I hope he consents!

GOVERNOR: He'll consent at once, you'll see! We'll settle the whole thing in fifteen minutes! Right here, here in front of *you*.

AGAZZI: What! Here, at my place?

SIRELLI: Do you think he'll be willing to bring his wife here?

GOVERNOR: Leave it to me! Yes, right here. Because I know that, otherwise, in your own minds you'll go on supposing that I—

AGAZZI: Oh, no, please! What a thought!

SIRELLI: That would never happen!

GOVERNOR: Go on, now! Knowing that I'm so sure that he's the one who's right, you would imagine that, to muzzle the whole affair, seeing that a civil servant is involved . . . —No, no; I want *you* to hear her also. (*Then, to Agazzi:*) Your wife?

AGAZZI: Is in the next room, with the other ladies . . .

GOVERNOR: Ha! You've set up a real conspiracy headquarters here . . .

SCENE FIVE

The foregoing, Centuri, Mr. Ponza.

CENTURI: May I?—Here is Mr. Ponza.

GOVERNOR: Thanks, Centuri. (*Mr. Ponza appears on the threshold.*) Come in, come in, my dear Ponza.

Mr. Ponza bows.

AGAZZI: Have a seat, please.

Mr. Ponza bows again and sits down.

GOVERNOR: You know these gentlemen . . . Sirelli . . .

Mr. Ponza rises and bows.

AGAZZI: Yes, I've already introduced him. My brother-in-law Laudisi.

Mr. Ponza bows.

GOVERNOR: I asked you in, my dear Ponza, to tell you that here, with my friends . . . (*He stops, noticing that, from his very first words, Mr. Ponza has exhibited great agitation and extreme excitement.*) You have something to say?

PONZA: Yes, Your Excellency: that I intend to ask for a transfer this very day.

GOVERNOR: But why? Just a while ago, you were talking to me, so gently . . .

PONZA: Your Excellency, I've been made the butt here of an unheard-of persecution!

GOVERNOR: Come now! Let's not exaggerate.

AGAZZI (*to Ponza*): Excuse me! When you say persecution, do you mean on my part?

PONZA: On everybody's! And that's why I'm leaving! I'm leaving, Your Excellency, because I cannot tolerate this dogged, fierce inquisition into my private life, which will end up jeopardizing or irreparably destroying a charitable effort that has cost me so much sorrow and so many sacrifices!—I revere that poor old lady more than if she were my mother, and here, yesterday, I found myself compelled to attack her with the most cruel violence. Now I have just found her in her apartment, in such a state of depression and nervousness—

AGAZZI (*interrupting him; calmly*): That's strange! Because, with us, she has always spoken with extreme calm. On the other hand, all the nervousness we've seen up to now has been in you, Mr. Ponza; and now is no exception!

PONZA: Because none of you know how you're making me suffer!

GOVERNOR: Now, now, calm yourself, my dear Ponza! What's wrong? I'm here! And you know with what trust and sympathy I've listened to your statements. Haven't I?

PONZA: Forgive me. You, yes. And I'm grateful to you for that, Your Excellency.

GOVERNOR: Well, then! Look here: you revere your poor mother-in-law as if she were your mother? If so, bear in mind that these friends of mine here are showing all this curiosity about the facts precisely because they, too, wish her well.

PONZA: But they're killing her, Your Excellency! And I've already pointed it out more than once!

GOVERNOR: Be patient. You'll see that they'll stop as soon as everything is cleared up. And that will be right away! There's nothing to it. — You possess the simplest and surest means to dispel all these gentlemen's doubts. Not mine, because I have none.

PONZA: But they refuse to believe me, no matter what I do!

AGAZZI: That's not true. — When you came here, after your mother-in-law's first call on us, to inform us that she was insane, we were all surprised, but we believed you. (*To the Governor:*) But immediately afterward — understand? — the lady came back —

GOVERNOR: Yes, yes, I know, you told me. (*Addressing Ponza again:*) She came to explain her own views, which you yourself are trying to keep alive in your mother-in-law's mind. You must be patient if a nagging doubt arises in the mind of someone who hears first you, then that poor lady. In the face of what your mother-in-law says, you see, these gentlemen don't feel they can any longer safely repose confidence in what *you* say, my dear Ponza. And so, it's clear. You and your mother-in-law — go! step aside for a moment! — *You*, Ponza, are sure that you're telling the truth, just as *I* am sure of it; you surely can have no objection if that truth is restated, here and now, by the only person who can confirm it, other than the two of you.

PONZA: Who is that?

GOVERNOR: Why, Mrs. Ponza!

PONZA: My wife? (*Vigorously, angrily:*) Oh, no! Never, Your Excellency!

GOVERNOR: And why not, tell me?

PONZA: Bring my wife here to give satisfaction to people who refuse to believe me?

GOVERNOR   (*quickly*): To me, if you please! — There's some difficulty?

PONZA: But, Your Excellency . . . No! My wife, no! Leave my wife alone! You can believe *me*!

GOVERNOR: No, see here, it's starting to look to me, too, in that case, as if you are trying your best not to be believed!

AGAZZI: Not to mention that he also tried in every way possible—even at the cost of being rude to my wife and daughter twice—to prevent his mother-in-law from coming here to talk.

PONZA   (*in an exasperated outburst*): But what do you all want of me? In God's name! That poor, sick old lady isn't enough for you? You want my wife here, too? Your Excellency, I can't put up with this tyranny! My wife doesn't leave my house! I don't bring her to grovel at anybody's feet! I'm satisfied if *you* believe me! And, besides, I'm going this instant to put in for my transfer out of here! (*Rises.*)

GOVERNOR   (*banging his fist on the desk*): Wait! First of all, Mr. Ponza, I can't countenance your taking such a tone with one of your superiors and with me, seeing that up to now I've spoken to you with such courtesy and deference. In the second place, I repeat that by this time you've raised some doubts even in my mind by your obstinate refusal to furnish a proof which *I* am asking you for, not somebody else, in your own interest, and in which I can see no harm!—My colleague and I are certainly fit to receive a lady's call . . . —or, if you wish, even to go to your place . . .

PONZA: So you're compelling me?

GOVERNOR: I repeat that I'm making this request for your own good. I could also demand it as your superior!

PONZA: All right. All right. If that's how it is, I'll bring my wife here, if only to put an end to this! But who will promise me that that poor woman won't see her?

GOVERNOR: Yes, of course . . . because she lives next door . . .

AGAZZI   (*quickly*): We could go into Mrs. Frola's apartment.

PONZA: No! It's all of you that I was talking about. I don't want another surprise that could have terrible consequences!

AGAZZI: Have no fear about us!

GOVERNOR: Or else—yes!—at your convenience you could bring Mrs. Ponza to my office.

PONZA: No, no—right away, here . . . right away . . . I'll stand guard over *her*, next door. I'm off at once, Your Excellency; and it will be over, it will be over! (*Exits in a frenzy through the back door.*)

SCENE SIX

The foregoing, except Mr. Ponza.

GOVERNOR: I confess to you that I didn't expect this opposition on his part.

AGAZZI: And you'll see that he's going to force his wife to say whatever *he* wants!

GOVERNOR: Oh, no! As for that, have no fear. *I* will interrogate her!

SIRELLI: But his constant touchiness, I ask you!

GOVERNOR: It's the first time—really!—the first time I've seen him like this.—Maybe the idea of bringing his wife here—

SIRELLI: Of letting her out of jail!—

GOVERNOR: Oh, that—his keeping her practically a prisoner—that can also be explained without resorting to the assumption that he's crazy.

SIRELLI: Excuse me, Your Excellency, you have never yet heard that poor lady.

AGAZZI: Right! He says that he keeps her that way because he fears for his mother-in-law.

GOVERNOR: But even if that weren't the reason: he might be jealous, and that's that.

SIRELLI: But even to the extent of not keeping a maid? He forces his wife to do all the housework herself!

AGAZZI: And *he* goes out marketing every morning!

CENTURI: Yes, it's true: I've seen him! A young boy helps him bring the food home—

SIRELLI: And is always made to wait outside the door!

GOVERNOR: My Lord, gentlemen: he himself complained about all that when he told me his situation.

LAUDISI: An unimpeachable source of information!

GOVERNOR: He does it to save money, Laudisi! He has to maintain two households. . .

SIRELLI: No, *we* think it's something else! Really, Your Excellency, do you believe that a second wife would put up with so much—

AGAZZI (*following up*): To do the lowliest household chores!—

SIRELLI (*continuing*): For the sake of a woman who used to be her husband's mother-in-law, but is a complete stranger to her?

AGAZZI: Come on, come on, now! Don't you think that's too much?

GOVERNOR: Too much, yes—

LAUDISI   (*interrupting*): For *just any* second wife!

GOVERNOR   (*quickly*): Let's admit it. Too much, yes.—And yet even
that, I tell you, can be perfectly explained, if not by the gen-
erosity of her nature, then, once again, by his jealousy. And
that he *is* jealous—whether he's crazy or not—I believe can't
possibly be denied.

*At this moment a shouting of mingled voices is heard from the living
room.*

AGAZZI: Hey! What's going on in there?

SCENE SEVEN

The foregoing, Amalia.

AMALIA   (*dashes in, thoroughly alarmed, through the door at stage left,
announcing*): Mrs. Frola!

AGAZZI: No! For God's sake, who sent for her?

AMALIA: No one! She came on her own!

GOVERNOR: No! For heaven's sake! Not now! Make her go away
again, Mrs. Agazzi!

AGAZZI: And at once! Don't let her in! You've got to stop her, no matter what! If he found her here, he'd really think it was an am-
bush!

SCENE EIGHT

The foregoing, Mrs. Frola, all the rest.

*Mrs. Frola enters, trembling, weeping, beseechingly, a handkerchief in
her hand, amid the throng of the others, who are all agitated.*

MRS. FROLA: Ladies and gentlemen, for pity's sake, for pity's sake! Tell
them, Your Honor!

AGAZZI   (*stepping forward, in great vexation*): I tell *you*, madam, to withdraw at once! Because for the moment you cannot remain here!

MRS. FROLA   (*bewildered*): Why? Why? (*To Amalia:*) I turn to you, my kind lady . . .

AMALIA: But look . . . look, the Governor is here . . .

MRS. FROLA: Oh! You, Your Excellency! For heaven's sake! I wanted to visit you!

GOVERNOR: No, have patience, Mrs. Frola! For now I can't hear you out. You must leave, leave here at once!

MRS. FROLA: Yes, I'll leave! I'll leave this very day! I'll leave town, Your Excellency! I'll leave for good!

AGAZZI: No, no, Mrs. Frola! Be so kind as to return to your apartment next door for a moment! Do me that favor! Then you can speak with His Excellency!

MRS. FROLA: But why? What's going on? What's going on?

AGAZZI   (*losing his patience*): Your son-in-law is on his way back here, that's what! Understand?

MRS. FROLA: Oh! Really? Well, then, yes . . . yes, I'll leave . . . I'll leave at once! All I wanted to tell you is: for pity's sake, put an end to this! You think you're helping me, and you're hurting me so much! I'll be forced to leave town if you keep this up; to go away this very day, so that *he* can be left in peace!—But what do you want, what do you want from him here now? What does he have to do when he comes here?—Oh, Your Excellency!

GOVERNOR: Nothing, Mrs. Frola, be calm! Be calm and go, please!

AMALIA: Go, Mrs. Frola, yes! Be good!

MRS. FROLA: Oh, Lord, Mrs. Agazzi, all of you are going to deprive me of the only joy, the only comfort, I had left: to see my daughter, if only from a distance! (*Starts to cry.*)

GOVERNOR: Who says so? You have no need to leave town! We just ask you to step outside now for a moment. Be calm!

MRS. FROLA: But I'm worried about *him*, about *him*, Your Excellency! I came here to implore everyone on *his* account, not on mine!

GOVERNOR: Yes, fine! And you may rest assured on his account, as well, I promise you. You'll see that everything will fall into place now.

MRS. FROLA: How? I see you all here attacking him furiously!

GOVERNOR: No, Mrs. Frola! It's not so! *I'm* on his side here. Be calm!

MRS. FROLA: Oh, thank you! That means you've understood . . .

GOVERNOR: Yes, yes, Mrs. Frola, I've understood.

MRS. FROLA: I've told all these ladies and gentlemen time and time
again: it's a misfortune we've already gotten over, and there's
no need to stir it up again.

GOVERNOR: Yes, fine, Mrs. Frola . . . I assure you I've understood!

MRS. FROLA: My daughter and I are contented living this way; she's
contented, too. And so . . . —Think about it, sir, think about
it . . . because, otherwise, there's nothing left for me but to
leave town, really, and never see her again, not even at a distance, like now . . . Leave him in peace, I beg of you!

*At this moment, a movement is visible among the throng; all make signs;
some look toward the door; a few quickly suppressed words are heard.*

VOICES: Oh, Lord . . . Here she is, here she is!

MRS. FROLA   (*noticing the general alarm and confusion, moaning in
bewilderment, trembling*): What's going on? What's going on?

SCENE NINE

The foregoing, Mrs. Ponza, then Mr. Ponza.

*All draw back on two sides, leaving an aisle for Mrs. Ponza, who advances
stiffly, in mourning, her face hidden by a thick, impenetrable black veil.*

MRS. FROLA   (*emitting a lacerating scream of frenetic joy*): Ah! Lina
. . . Lina. . . Lina . . .

*She dashes toward the veiled woman and clings to her with the fervor of
a mother who has not embraced her daughter for years and years. But at
the same time, from inside, are heard the cries of Mr. Ponza, who immediately thereupon dashes onstage.*

PONZA: Giulia! . . . Giulia! . . . Giulia! . . . (*On hearing his cries, Mrs.
Ponza stiffens in the encircling arms of Mrs. Frola. Mr. Ponza,
coming closer, immediately sees his mother-in-law embracing
his wife so desperately, and, in a rage, he rails at the others:*)

Ah! I said so! That's how you took a mean advantage of my good faith?

MRS. PONZA (*turning her veiled head, as if with austere solemnity*): Don't be afraid! Don't be afraid! Go away, both of you.

PONZA (*quietly, lovingly, to Mrs. Frola*): Let's go, yes, let's go . . .

MRS. FROLA (*who has broken the embrace of her own accord, trembling all over, humbly, immediately echoes his words, solicitously*): Yes, yes . . . let's go, dear, let's go . . .

And both of them, arm in arm, stroking each other, each weeping in his own way, exit, whispering affectionate words to each other. Silence. After watching the two make a total exit, the others, alarmed and moved, now give their attention again to the veiled woman.

MRS. PONZA (*after looking at them through her veil, says with sepulchral solemnity*): What more can you want of me after this, ladies and gentlemen? Here, as you see, lies a misfortune that must remain hidden, because only in that way can the remedy found by a spirit of charity continue to be effective.

GOVERNOR (*touched*): And we wish to respect that spirit of charity, Mrs. Ponza. But we'd like you to tell us—

MRS. PONZA (*slowly and distinctly*): What? The truth? It is only this: that I really am the daughter of Mrs. Frola—

ALL (*with a sigh of contentment*): Ah!

MRS. PONZA (*joining in quickly; as above*): And also the second wife of Mr. Ponza—

ALL (*amazed and disappointed; meekly*): Oh! But how?

MRS. PONZA (*joining in quickly; as above*): Yes—and for myself, no one! I am no one!

GOVERNOR: Oh, no, Mrs. Ponza: for yourself, you must be one or the other!

MRS. PONZA: No. For myself, I am the woman that I am believed to be.

For an instant she looks at everyone through her veil; then exits. Silence.

LAUDISI: And that, ladies and gentlemen, is the voice of truth! (*He looks all around with an expression of challenging mockery.*) Satisfied? (*He bursts out laughing:*) Ha! ha! ha! ha!

CURTAIN